Thea Stilton

3 in 1

PAPERCUTZ

Thea Stilton

GRAPHIC NOVELS AVAILABLE FROM PAPERCUTZ

...ALSO AVAILABLE WHEREVER E-BOOKS ARE SOLD!

#1
"The Secret of Whale Island"

#2
"Revenge of the Lizard Club"

#3
"The Treasure of the Viking Ship"

#4
"Catching the Giant Wave"

#5
"The Secret of the Waterfall in the Woods"

#6
"The Thea Sisters and the Mystery at Sea"

#7
"A Song for the Thea Sisters"

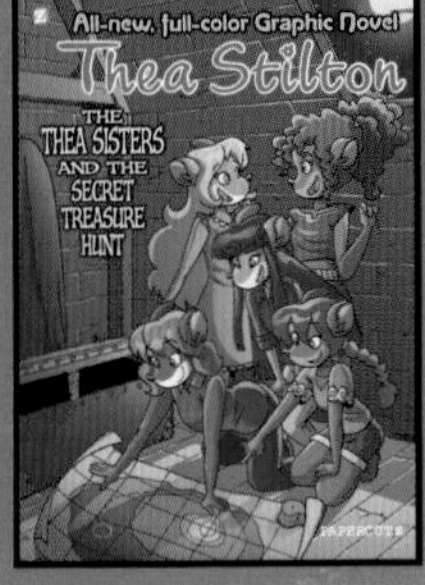

#8
"The Thea Sisters and the Secret Treasure Hunt"

#8
"The Thea Sisters and the Secret Treasure Hunt"

#1
Thea Stilton 3 IN 1

#2
Thea Stilton 3 IN 1

See more at papercutz.com

Thea Stilton

3 IN 1 #2

By Thea Stilton

"Catching the Giant Wave"

"The Secret of the Waterfall in the Woods"

"Mystery at Sea"

New York

"Catching the Giant Wave"
© 2009 Edizioni Piemme © 2018 Mondadori Libri S.p.A. for PIEMME, Italia
International rights © 2009 Atlantyca S.p.A.
© 2014–for this work in English language by Papercutz
Original Title: "Aspettando l'onda gigante"
Text by Thea Stilton
Text Coordination by Sarah Rossi (Atlantyca S.p.A.)
Editorial Coordination by Patrizia Puricelli and Serena Bellani
Artistic Coordination by Flavio Ferron with the assistance of Tommaso Valsechi
Editing by Yellowhale and Robyn Chapman
Editing Coordination and Artwork Supervision by Stefania Bitta and Maryam Funicelli
Editing Associate by Michael Petranek
Script Supervision by Francesco Artibani
Story by Francesco Artibani and Caterina Mognato
Design by Arianna Rea
Art by Michela Frare
Color by Ketty Formaggio
With the assistance of Marta Lorini
Production Coordination by Beth Scorzato
Cover of THEA STILTON #4 by Arianna Rea (design), Michela Frare (art), and Ketty Formaggio (color)

"The Secret of the Waterfall in the Woods"
© 2015 Atlantyca S.p.A
© 2015–for this work in English language by Papercutz
Text by Thea Stilton
Project Supervision by Alessandra Berello (Atlantyca S.p.A.)
Script by Francesco Savino and Leonardo Favia
Translation by Nanette McGuinness
Production by Dawn Guzzo
Editing by Carol M. Burrell
Associate Editing by Bethany Bryan
Art by Ryan Jampole
Color by Mindy Indy with the assistance of Matt Herms
Lettering by Wilson Ramos Jr. and Grace Lu
Cover of THEA STILTON #5 by Ryan Jampole (art) and JayJay Jackson (color)

"The Thea Sisters and the Mystery at Sea"
© 2016 Atlantyca S.p.A
© 2016–for this work in English language by Papercutz
Text by Thea Stilton
Project Supervision by Alessandra Berello (Atlantyca S.p.A.)
Script by Francesco Savino
Translation by Nanette McGuinness
Production by Dawn Guzzo
Editing by Rachel Gluckstern
Art by Ryan Jampole
Color by Dave Tanguay, Laurie E. Smith, and Matteo Baldrighi
Lettering by Wilson Ramos Jr.
Cover of THEA STILTON #6 by Ryan Jampole (art) and Matt Herms (color)

Editorial supervision by Alessandra Berello and Chiara Richelmi (Atlantyca S.p.A.)
Editorial Interns – Grant Frederick, Karr Antunes
Assistant Managing Editor – Jeff Whitman
Jim Salicrup
Editor-in-Chief

ISBN: 978-1-5458-0531-2
Printed in Korea
February 2019

Papercutz books may be purchased for business or promotional use.
For information on bulk purchases, please contact Macmillan Corporate and Premium Sales Department at (800) 221-7945 x5442.

Distributed by Macmillan
First Printing

CATCHING THE GIANT WAVE

FINALLY A LOVELY DAY OF SUN ON *Whale Island!* NICKY JUMPS AT THE CHANCE TO TEACH PAMELA AND PAULINA HOW TO SURF.

THE ROUGH, CHOPPY SEA AT VERY WINDY POINT CALLS TO HER IRRESISTIBLY-- SINCE SHE'S USED TO THE OCEAN WAVES OF AUSTRALIA!

DON'T STIFFEN UP, PAM! LOOSE LEGS AND AN IRON WILL!

PULVERIZED PISTONS!

LOOK, VIOLET! PAM'S FACING HER FIRST WAVE!

EEEH-- -GLUB!-

FWOOSH

-SPLUT!-

HA! HA! HA! YOU LOOK LIKE A SEAL, PAM! **HEE! HEE!**

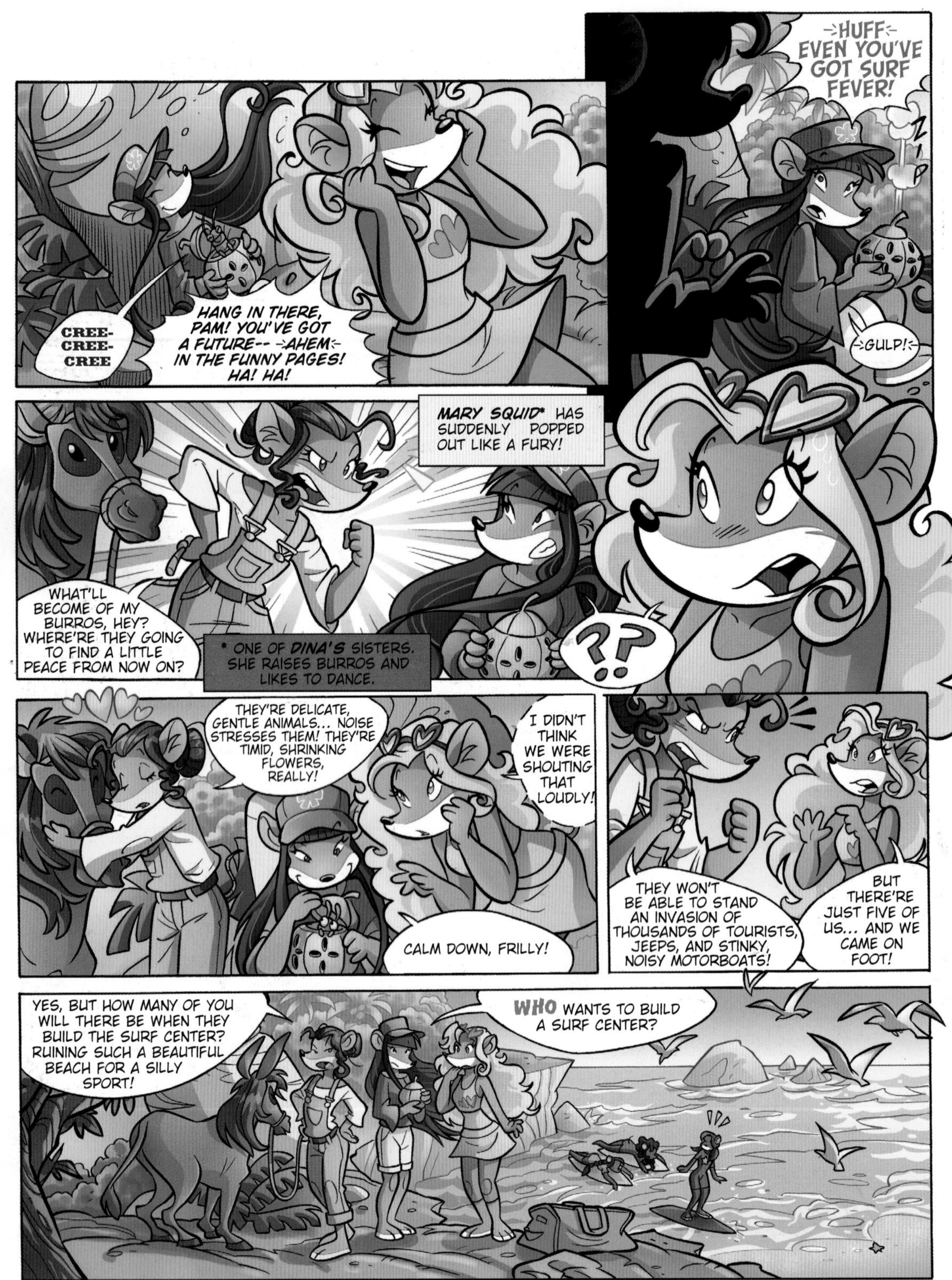
CREE-CREE-CREE
HANG IN THERE, PAM! YOU'VE GOT A FUTURE-- ⇾AHEM⇽ IN THE FUNNY PAGES! HA! HA!
⇾HUFF⇽ EVEN YOU'VE GOT SURF FEVER!
ZIP
⇾GULP!⇽
MARY SQUID* HAS SUDDENLY POPPED OUT LIKE A FURY!
WHAT'LL BECOME OF MY BURROS, HEY? WHERE'RE THEY GOING TO FIND A LITTLE PEACE FROM NOW ON?
* ONE OF DINA'S SISTERS. SHE RAISES BURROS AND LIKES TO DANCE.
??
THEY'RE DELICATE, GENTLE ANIMALS... NOISE STRESSES THEM! THEY'RE TIMID, SHRINKING FLOWERS, REALLY!
I DIDN'T THINK WE WERE SHOUTING THAT LOUDLY!
CALM DOWN, FRILLY!
THEY WON'T BE ABLE TO STAND AN INVASION OF THOUSANDS OF TOURISTS, JEEPS, AND STINKY, NOISY MOTORBOATS!
BUT THERE'RE JUST FIVE OF US... AND WE CAME ON FOOT!
YES, BUT HOW MANY OF YOU WILL THERE BE WHEN THEY BUILD THE SURF CENTER? RUINING SUCH A BEAUTIFUL BEACH FOR A SILLY SPORT!
WHO WANTS TO BUILD A SURF CENTER?

MARY HEARD ABOUT THE NEW CENTER FROM HER SISTER DINA. SO *THE THEA SISTERS* DECIDE TO GET THE EXPLANATION STRAIGHT FROM HER...
IT'S THE MAYOR'S INITIATIVE! HE WANTS TO COMPETE WITH ***VISSIA DE VISSEN*** AND HER SURF CLUB.
REALLY?!
I DON'T EVEN KNOW WHO THE MAYOR IS...
THEY JUST ELECTED HIM! IT'S ***ROMEO, VINCE GUYMOUSE'S*** COUSIN!
OH, THE OWNER OF THE RESTAURANT ***"CHEZ ROMEO!"***
REALLY A NICE FUTURE!
ROMEO EXAGGERATES, BUT HE'S NOT BAD.
THE OLD CITY COUNCIL WAS AN OUTDATED INSTITUTION! THE ISLAND NEEDS A **MODERN** ADMINISTRATION!
BUT WHY ELECT HIM, PRECISELY?
ROMEO'S TRAVELLED THE WORLD! HE'S SEEN HOW THINGS WORK ELSEWHERE! AND NOW THAT HE'S BACK, HE WANTS TO "LAUNCH OUR ISLAND INTO THE FUTURE!"... OR AT LEAST THAT'S WHAT HE SAYS...
NO ONE ELSE WANTED TO TAKE ON THE JOB!
"ROMEO GUYMOUSE IS A MAYOR WITH LOTS OF IDEAS AND INITIATIVES!"
WE'LL TRANSFORM WHALE ISLAND INTO A **PARADISE** FOR THE RICH FROM AROUND THE WORLD!
IF ONLY RICH FOLKS STAY HERE, WHERE'LL OUR FISHERMEN GO?
EXCLUSIVE HOTELS! ADVANCED TECHNOLOGY! VERY DISTINGUISHED CLIENTELE!

Chez Romeo
HURRAY FOR MY COUSIN!
BRAVO FOR THE MAYOR!
LET'S ALL GO INSIDE TO CELEBRATE!
I'LL STAY FOR A MINUTE, BUT EATING AT HIS PLACE? YUCK!

ROMEO'S NOT A BAD RODENT AT HEART!
HE'S JUST A BIT TOO MUCH OF, HOW SHOULD I SAY IT... AN ***OPTIMIST*** AND A ***DREAMER!***

BUT EVEN ROMEO GUYMOUSE HAS HIS PROBLEMS!
MY RESTAURANT IS ***VERY BEAUTIFUL*** BUT... IT'S ALWAYS EMPTY!
MMM... HER CHEESE CANAPÉS GO RIGHT TO MY **HEART!**
I CAN'T FIND A COOK WHO MEASURES UP! AH, IF ONLY ***MIDGE*** WORKED FOR ME...

QUICK, KID, GO TO THE FLORIST RIGHT AWAY! BUY A BUNCH OF ROSES AND SEND THEM TO MOUSEFORD ACADEMY... TO **MISS MIDGE WHALE**, FROM ME!
-GULP!- YES, SIR!
HEY! WHO WANTS TO ASK FOR THE HAND OF YOUR DAUGHTER MIDGE?
-HMPH!-
VISSIA DE VISSEN'S DREAMS ARE MUCH MORE **PRACTICAL** THAN ROMEO'S...
MY SURF CLUB OPENS IN A WEEK! THE MOST LUXURIOUS IN THE WORLD!
AND THIS IS JUST THE BEGINNING! NOW IT'S TIME TO **EXPAND** MY RANGE OF OPERATIONS!
WELCOME, MR. MAYOR!

WHAT'S THE MAYOR DOING ON VISSIA'S YACHT?
MY FELLOW CITIZENS ARE TRADITIONALISTS. PROJECTS LIKE THIS ALARM THEM! I DON'T KNOW IF--
TSK! STILL HESITATING?!
SO, MY DEAR ROMEO, WILL THERE BE A SURF CENTER ON DONKEY BEACH OR NOT?
I JUST SHELLED OUT BILLIONS TO MAKE WINDY ISLAND INTO THE MOST EXCLUSIVE, SURFING-EST RESORT IN THE WORLD!
I EVEN HAD A REEF BUILT SO THE WAVES WILL BE PERFECT YEAR ROUND!
–COUGH! COUGH!– THERE'LL BE ONE! –COUGH!– THERE'LL BE ONE...
BUT MY ISLAND WILL ONLY HOUSE A FEW PRIVILEGED PEOPLE! MASS TOURISM IS WHAT WILL BRING IN BIG PROFITS!
THAT'S WHY I WANT YOU TO BUILD A SURF CENTER ON WHALE ISLAND! TO HOUSE THE CROWDS OF TOURISTS... WHO WILL BRING IN SO MUCH MONEY!
YES. AHEM... OF COURSE!
I HAD MY EXPERTS DRAW UP PLANS!
ALAN, THE SLIDES!
FIRST, WE'LL CONSTRUCT AN ARTIFICIAL REEF HERE, TOO!
SECOND, WE'LL CREATE A BIG... NO, A HUGE HOTEL ON RAM PLAIN!

THIRD, WE'LL BUILD SEASIDE FACILITIES ON DONKEY BEACH!
CLAP CLAP CLAP
SPLENDID!

BUT... APPROVAL OF A PROJECT LIKE THIS REQUIRES A POPULAR REFERENDUM...
WELL? THEN HAVE ONE RIGHT AWAY!

WHALE ISLAND'S RESIDENTS WOULD NEVER ALLOW A STRANGER TO PUT HER PAWS IN THEIR ISLAND'S BUSINESS!
WITH MY MONEY, YOU'LL BE SURE TO WIN!

OUR AGREEMENT WILL REMAIN SECRET, OF COURSE!
IT'S BETTER THAT WAY! I'VE MADE IT SEEM THAT THE SURF CENTER IS MY IDEA... TO GIVE YOU COMPETITION!

PERFECT! HA! HA! HA!

NEWS OF WHALE ISLAND'S SURF CENTER REFERENDUM EVEN REACHED MOUSEFORD ACADEMY!
WE ALSO WANT TO BUILD A SURF CENTER ON WHALE ISLAND...
HEE! HEE! HEE!
HEH! HEH!
?

... BUT ALL THE VIPS WILL BE AT MY MOTHER'S CENTER, ON WINDY ISLAND!
ALL... EXCEPT FOR THE REAL SURFING CHAMPIONS!

YOU'RE WRONG! DO YOU KNOW WHO'S GOING TO OPEN THE SURF CLUB? NONE OTHER THAN GARY MOON!

THEY'RE EVEN GOING TO FILM COMMERCIALS... WITH JUST GARY AND ME!
HEE! HEE! HEE!
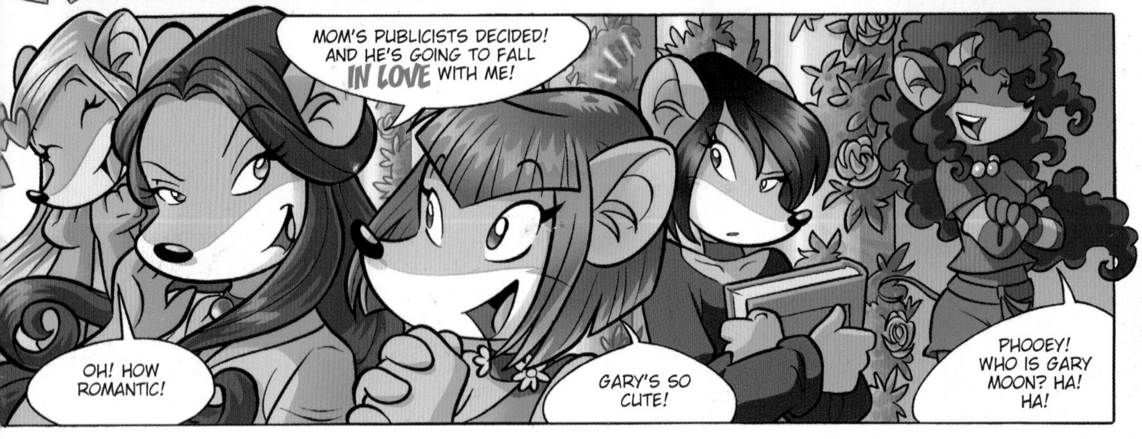
MOM'S PUBLICISTS DECIDED! AND HE'S GOING TO FALL IN LOVE WITH ME!
OH! HOW ROMANTIC!
GARY'S SO CUTE!
PHOOEY! WHO IS GARY MOON? HA! HA!

HEY?! WHAT'S GOTTEN INTO YOU? AND WHAT'S UP WITH NICKY?
GARY MOON'S THE AUSTRALIAN SURFING CHAMPION! NICKY'S OBSESSED WITH HIM... DIDN'T YOU KNOW?
SMAK
OH, NOW I GET IT! HE'S THE GUY ON THE POSTER IN HER ROOM!
WHAT AN AWFUL BLOW, TO FIND OUT HE'LL BE VANILLA'S GUEST. POOR NICKY!
WHY WOULD GARY CARE ABOUT A FLIRT LIKE VANILLA?
WOW! HE'S REALLY CUTE!
DO YOU WANT ME TO GET HIS AUTOGRAPH, NICKY?
OH, PAM, THAT WOULD BE FANTASTIC!
LEAVE IT TO AN EXPERT! YOU'LL SEE. I'LL EVEN MANAGE TO GET YOU A DEDICATION!

AND THE REFERENDUM? DID YOU FORGET ABOUT IT, KIDS? WE'VE GOT TO SEE THAT THE MAYOR'S PLAN DOESN'T PASS!
RIGHT! BUT, HOW?
LET'S ASK THE ***HEADMASTER...!***
SO, A LITTLE LATER...
I SHARE YOUR CONCERNS, KIDS, BUT MOUSEFORD ACADEMY'S CHARTER DOESN'T ALLOW US TO INTERFERE WITH ISLAND POLITICS!
OH...
YOU'RE SO WELL RESPECTED ON THE ISLAND...
I'M SORRY, BUT MY PAWS ARE TIED!
SO, WHO CAN HELP US NOW?
PROFESSOR VAN KRAKEN WILL CERTAINLY LEND US A PAW!
YES, BUT HIS LANGUAGE IS TOO... TECHNICAL.
YOU MEAN, NO ONE CAN UNDERSTAND HIM!
ROMEO GUYMOUSE, ON THE OTHER HAND, SURE KNOWS HOW TO GET PEOPLE TO LISTEN!
YOU'RE RIGHT! OUR MAYOR'S A GREAT SPEAKER!
AND HE'S SO DISTINGUISHED! A REAL GENTLEMOUSE!
I'M AFRAID THE BATTLE IS LOST BEFORE WE START...
NO, NO, AND ONCE AGAIN, NO! OUR BATTLE ISN'T LOST. OUR BATTLE IS **RIGHTEOUS!**

"AGREED. PROFESSOR VAN KRAKEN ISN'T A GREAT SPEAKER, BUT HE CAN ALWAYS LEND US A PAW."
I'M WITH YOU, KIDS!
FIRST OF ALL, LET'S GO SEE WHAT MS. DE VISSEN HAS DONE TO THE SEA FLOOR.
ENCLOSED SPACES AREN'T SO GOOD FOR ME... THE LAST TIME WAS TORTURE...
THERE'S NO OTHER WAY TO INSPECT THE ARTIFICIAL REEF.
UMM... THE SUBMERSIBLE IS SO TINY AND I...
DON'T WORRY, NICKY! WE DON'T ALL NEED TO GO!
I'LL STAY ON DRY LAND WITH YOU!
I DON'T WANT TO GO UNDERWATER EITHER. THE HUMIDITY WILL MAKE MY HAIR ALL FRIZZY!
TAKE THE KEY TO MY ATV! GO SEE WHAT'S HAPPENING IN TOWN!
HERE'S WHAT'S HAPPENING IN TOWN!
HEAD INTO THE FUTURE WITH ROMEO!
CAREENING KANGAROOS! THE MAYOR'S DOING THINGS IN STYLE!

LOOK AT ALL THOSE POSTERS!
WHERE'D HE FIND THE MONEY FOR A CAMPAIGN LIKE THIS?
I'M LOOKING INTO THE FUTURE
YOU KNOW WHAT I SAY? I SMELL A RAT HERE!
THERE WAS NO LACK OF SURPRISES UNDERWATER, EITHER!
THE REEF IS GIGANTIC!
WHAT'S THAT THING MADE OF, PROFESSOR?
THEY'RE ENORMOUS SACKS OF SAND, PAM! BUT IT'S TOO BIG. I CAN'T FIGURE OUT ITS EXACT CONFIGURATION.
WE COULD TAKE PICTURES OF IT AND MEASURE IT!
YOU'RE RIGHT, PAULINA! THAT WILL SERVE AS ACCURATE DOCUMENTATION! THEN I'LL CONTACT SOME EXPERTS ABOUT IT!

THAT EVENING, AFTER RETURNING FROM THEIR RESPECTIVE "MISSIONS," THE THEA SISTERS WERE SUMMONED TO THE ACADEMY'S GREAT HALL, ALONG WITH ALL THE OTHER STUDENTS...

I CAN ALREADY IMAGINE VANILLA'S FACE! ***HA! HA!***

WHAT?! REALLY, I JUST WANTED...

WELL, ACTUALLY, INTRODUCING HIM TO NICKY IS MUCH BETTER THAN AN AUTOGRAPH!

OF COURSE, VIC'S COMPLETELY FLIPPED! HE ALWAYS MANAGES TO SURPRISE ME!

SMACK

THE NEXT MORNING, ON WINDY ISLAND...

HOW DO I LOOK, MOM?

YOU LOOK SCRUMPTIOUS, DAUGHTER! YOU'LL LEAVE OUR CHAMPION BREATHLESS!

NOW CUT THAT OUT! LET HIM BREATHE!
???
WELCOME TO WINDY ISLAND, GARY!
THANKS, MISS...?
I'M VANILLA DE VISSEN!
THANKS, MISS VANILLA!
CLAP CLAP
A REAL STAR!
SHE'S SO LOVELY! AND WHAT A SPITFIRE!
CLAP CLAP
I'M JACK CAMERON, GARY MOON'S AGENT. I'M AT YOUR SERVICE, MS. DE VISSEN!
OH, IT'S JUST YOU!
IS IT CLEAR WHAT GARY IS SUPPOSED TO DO? I'M NOT JUST PAYING HIM TO STAR IN THE COMMERCIAL!
NO PROBLEM! HE DOES EVERYTHING I TELL HIM!
MY PUBLICITY TEAM SUGGESTED WE INVENT A LOVE STORY BETWEEN GARY AND MY DAUGHTER!
MY LITTLE ONE IS A FAN OF HIS, BUT... DON'T LET GARY GET THE WRONG IDEA!
DON'T WORRY, MA'AM... I REALLY DON'T THINK VANILLA IS HIS TYPE...
OF COURSE, SHE'LL BREAK GARY'S HEART! BUT I HAVE OTHER PROJECTS IN MIND FOR MY LITTLE CHEESE PUFF!
?!

THEY'VE GOT THE SET ALL READY TO GO! ALRIGHT, LET'S FILM RIGHT AWAY!
LET'S TAKE A WALK, JUST YOU AND ME! THE ISLAND'S SO ROMANTIC...
IT'S BEEN 24 HOURS SINCE I'VE BEEN IN THE WATER! STELLA'S VERY DEHYDRATED!
STELLA? WHO'S STELLA?
MY SURFBOARD! I CALL HER... STELLA!
HMPH...
IF VANILLA WANTS TO STAY AT THE CHAMP'S SIDE, SHE'LL HAVE TO PART WITH HER NICE CLOTHES AND... GET IN THE WATER!
FILM NOW? FINE WITH ME!
BRING ME MY SURF SUIT!
THE WATER'S FINE! HURRY UP, VANILLA!
-OOF!- THE WATER MUST BE FREEZING!
READY ON THE SET... ACTION!

LOOSEN UP, VANILLA! DON'T BE AFRAID!
-GASP!-
SPLASH
HELPPP!
VANILLAAA!
HA! HA! HA! WHAT AN ARTIST!
OH, CUT IT OUT! DON'T BE JEALOUS OF YOUR SISTER!
ME, *JEALOUS?!* YOU'RE THE ONE WHO DOTES ON HER!

IN THE EVENING, THE LUXURIOUS *SURF CLUB* COMES ALIVE WITH GUESTS FOR THE OPENING...

WHAT LUXURY!

FLASH

FLASH

WHAT A MAGNIFICENT BUFFET!

WOW! SO MANY PEOPLE!

BUT WHERE'D THEY HIDE WONDERFUL GARY?

LOOK FOR VANILLA AND YOU'RE SURE TO FIND HIM...

COME ON, NICKY! DON'T BE SO SHY... HE'S JUST A GUY!

HEY, THERE! YOU FINALLY GOT HERE!

WHY? WERE YOU WAITING FOR US?

COME WITH ME, NICKY! VANILLA'S MOVED AWAY... WE HAVE TO TAKE ADVANTAGE OF IT!

HUH?!

HEY! WHERE'RE YOU TAKING HER?!

HEY! WATCH WHERE YOU'RE GOING!
HERE'S THE SOLUTION TO YOUR PROBLEM! HER NAME IS NICKY AND SHE'S A WHIRLWIND ON THE WAVES!
??
SHE CAN BE VANILLA'S STUNT DOUBLE!
PERFECT! THAT WAY, YOUR SISTER WILL STAY CALM AND DRY AND... THERE'LL BE NO MORE HYSTERICS!
PLEASED TO MEET YOU, NICKY!
M-ME, TOO! UM, I MEAN... I'M P-PLEASED, TOO... COUGH... I-I'M AUSTRALIAN, TOO!
A FELLOW SURFING COMPATRIOT! FANTASTIC!
YEAH!
R-RIGHT! F-FANTASTIC!
WHAT'D I TELL YOU? VIC'S NOT AS BAD AS HE SEEMS AFTER ALL! IT WAS A GOOD IDEA TO TALK TO HIM!
I'M SO THRILLED FOR NICKY!

STOP STARING AT THEM! LET'S DIVE INTO THE BUFFET!
BUT I WANT TO SEE...
IT'S A GALA EVENING AND AN EVENING OF SPECIAL ENCOUNTERS AT THE SURF CLUB...
MMM..., THESE CANAPÉS ARE DELICIOUS!
NOT AS DELICIOUS AS YOURS, MISS WHALE!
YOUR CHEESE CANAPÉS ARE PEARLS OF DELIGHT THAT GO FROM THE STOMACH STRAIGHT TO THE HEART!
OOOH! YOU FLATTER ME, MR. ROMEO!
AH, IF I COULD ONLY FIND THE COURAGE...
TO DO WHAT?
OH, HEAVENS! HE WANTS TO ASK FOR MY HAND IN MARRIAGE!
MISS WHALE! WOULD YOU BECOME... MY CHEF?
CH-CH-EF?!

CHEF! HMPH!
ERK?!

THE EVENING STILL HAS OTHER SURPRISES IN STORE!
NICKY!

WHAT'S THAT GIRL DOING WITH GARY?!
CALM DOWN, LITTLE SIS! EVERYTHING'S OKAY!

SHE'S SAVING YOU FROM THE WAVES, 'NILLA!
SHE'S GOING TO BE YOUR STUNT DOUBLE IN THE TOUGH SCENE! EVEN MOM AGREES!
YOU WERE THE ONE WHO INTRODUCED HIM TO HER, RIGHT?

GRRR... YOU SNAKE!
CRASH

MOM! YOU CAN'T ALLOW IT! IT'S NOT FAIR!
?

THEY WANT TO REPLACE ME IN THE COMMERCIAL! THEY GOT NICKY TO TAKE MY PLACE!
NO ONE IS REPLACING YOU, SWEETHEART! BUT THAT WAVE IS TOO **DANGEROUS** FOR YOU! THEY'LL JUST FILM YOU IN THE **FOREGROUND!**

ALL THE BIG STARS USE STUNT DOUBLES! DO YOU WANT TO BE LESS THAN THEM, PERHAPS?
HMM...

WHAT'S GOING ON, VANILLA?
WHY'S GARY TALKING TO NICKY?
SHE'S SO DULL...
!

NICKY'S GOING TO BE MY STUNT DOUBLE! ALL THE BIG STARS HAVE ONE... DON'T YOU KNOW?

COME ON, GARY... THE PHOTOGRAPHERS ARE CALLING FOR US!
AGAIN?

SEE YOU TOMORROW...
SEE YOU TOMORROW...
WELLLL!
JUST A STUNT DOUBLE, RIGHT?

THE NEXT DAY, NICKY AND GARY RIDE THE WAVES TOGETHER...
HE'S RESERVED: HE DOESN'T LIKE CROWDS AND ONLY FEELS AT EASE ON HIS SURFBOARD...
GARY
I'LL LEAD YOU, NICKY! TRUST ME!
... BUT IT DOESN'T TAKE MANY WORDS TO KNOW THEY BOTH LIKE THE SAME THINGS!
THANKS, VIC!
DON'T MENTION IT! AGGRAVATING VANILLA IS MY FAVORITE SPORT!
HMPH!
DON'T WORRY! KEEP IN MIND, YOU'LL BE GARY'S GUIDE FOR THE WHOLE DAY TOMORROW!
NO SCHOOL TOMORROW? OH, MOM, YOU'RE GREAT!
SMACK
I'VE PLANNED EVERYTHING, BECAUSE PAYING ATTENTION TO EVERY DETAIL LEADS TO PERFECTION! EVEN MY WAVES ARE WORKING WONDERFULLY!

BEAUTIFUL WAVES BUT... PERHAPS A BIT TOO BIG FOR A CALM DAY!
HELLO, ENGINEER O'CONNOR! DID YOU GET THE MEASUREMENTS FOR THE WINDY ISLAND REEF?
YES, PROFESSOR VAN KRAKEN. I GOT THEM BUT... THEY'RE ALL WRONG!
I ASSURE YOU, THEY'RE EXACT TO THE MILLIMETER!
IMPOSSIBLE! I DREW UP THE PLANS MYSELF... ALTHOUGH I DIDN'T WATCH THE CONSTRUCTION WORK AFTERWARDS.
THE MEASUREMENTS YOU SENT ARE ROUGHLY DOUBLE MINE!
OBVIOUSLY, THEY MODIFIED THE PLANS!
THAT'S ABSURD! INSANE! AN ARTIFICIAL REEF THAT BIG WILL CAUSE A DISASTER! WE MUST TEAR IT DOWN IMMEDIATELY!
UNDER THE STARRY SKY, THOSE DANGEROUS WAVES SEEM PERFECT TO NICKY AND GARY AFTER A DAY OF FILMING...
AND THIS MOMENT IN THEIR LIVES ALSO SEEMS PERFECT!
THAT SHOULD BE GARY AND ME! YOU'LL PAY FOR THIS, NICKY!

ON MONDAY MORNING, IT WAS HARD FOR NICKY TO GET BACK TO FOCUSING ON HER STUDIES...
AND EVEN GARY HAS HIS HEAD IN THE CLOUDS! HE LETS HIMSELF BE DRAGGED AROUND WHALE ISLAND, BUT HE DOESN'T SEE ANYTHING THAT'S GOING ON AROUND HIM!
SMILE FOR THE PHOTOGRAPHERS, GARY!
FLOSH
HUH? WHAT'D YOU SAY?
VISSIA PLANNED OUT THE CHAMPION'S EVERY STEP...
GARY MOON! WELCOME TO WHALE ISLAND!
... IN AGREEMENT WITH JACK CAMERON, HIS AGENT!
HURRAY FOR SURFING!
GARY, YOU'RE GREAT!
GARY
Gary Moon
Gary
YES ON THE SURE CEN

CLAP CLAP
IT'S GREAT! IT'LL BRING LOADS OF TOURISTS TO OUR ISLAND!
CLAP CLAP
CLAP
TO WINDY ISLAND, YOU MEAN!

TO OUR ISLAND TOO, IF WE BUILD A SURF CENTER!
I'M AGAINST THAT SURF CENTER AND THE ARTIFICIAL REEF! THE WAVES AT VERY WINDY POINT ARE ALREADY TOO BIG!

YOU FISHERMEN ARE AGAINST PROGRESS!
AND YOU SHOPKEEPERS ONLY THINK ABOUT MONEY!

STOP FIGHTING! THERE'S THE TV CREW! YOU'RE ON CAMERA!

HI, DINA! CAN YOU SEE ME?

TIME PASSES VERY SLOWLY AT MOUSEFORD ACADEMY AS NICKY WAITS FOR THE HOUR OF THEIR DATE TO ARRIVE...
I'LL BE ABLE TO GET FREE AT EIGHT O'CLOCK... I PROMISE!
GARY'S ON TV!
-OOF!- ROMEO GUYMOUSE WILL GET LOADS OF VOTES, JUST FROM GARY'S APPEARANCE!
IT'S ALL PUBLICITY IN FAVOR OF THE SURF CENTER!
DO YOU LIKE OUR SEA, GARY? IS IT ALRIGHT FOR SURFING?
OH, IT'S REALLY MAGNIFICENT!
DID YOU CATCH THAT? NOW EVERYONE WILL THINK HE SUPPORTS THE MAYOR'S PROJECT!
BUT GARY DOESN'T KNOW ANYTHING ABOUT IT! HE JUST GOT HERE FROM AUSTRALIA!
WHEN YOU'RE FAMOUS, YOU HAVE TO PAY ATTENTION TO WHAT YOU SAY!
GARY ONLY SAID THAT THE SEA IS GORGEOUS... AND IT'S TRUE!
WHAT A CUTE COUPLE! THEY'RE REALLY MADE FOR EACH OTHER!
HE'S FALLEN FOR HER! YOU CAN READ IT IN HIS FACE!
HUH?!

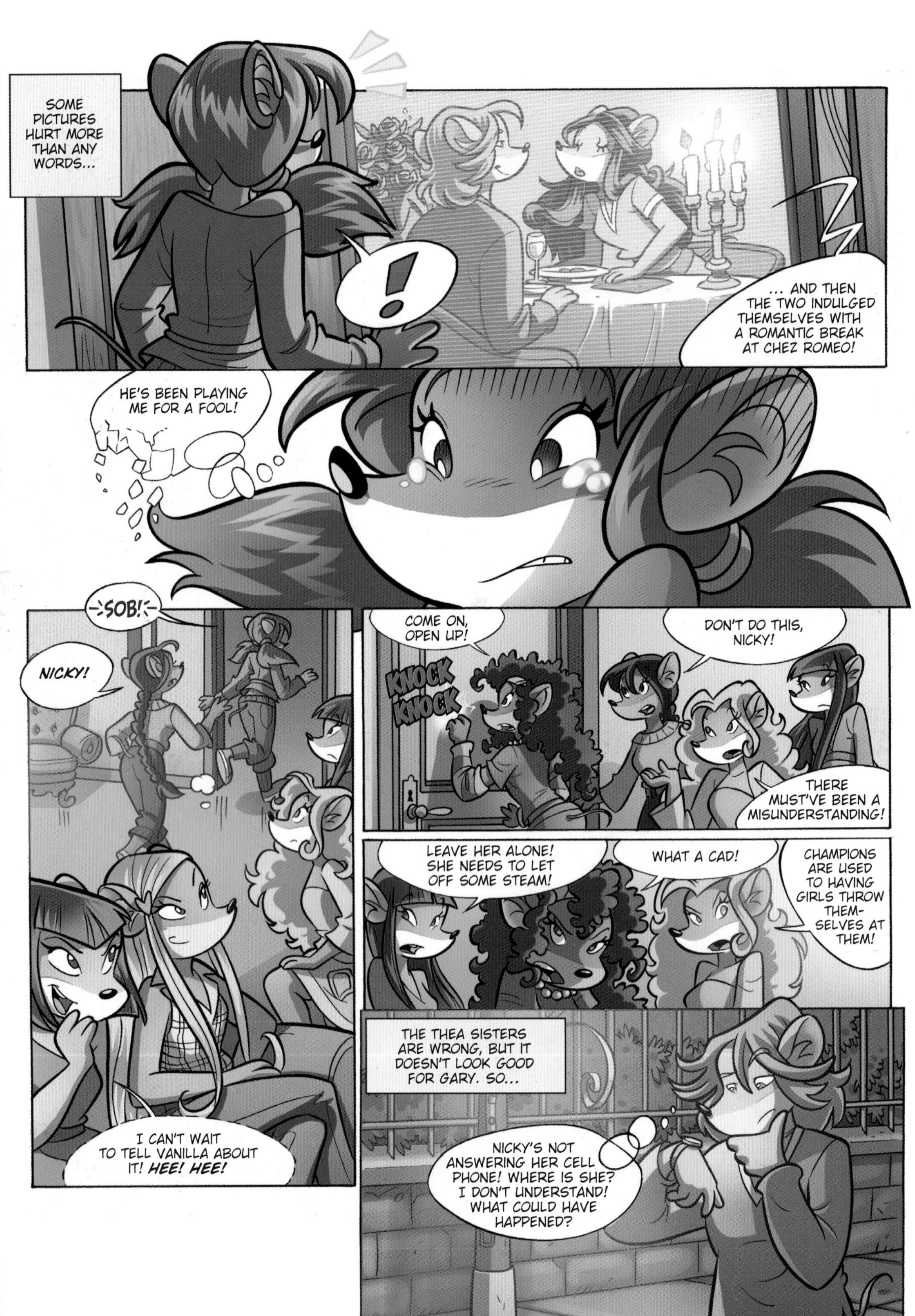
SOME PICTURES HURT MORE THAN ANY WORDS...
!
... AND THEN THE TWO INDULGED THEMSELVES WITH A ROMANTIC BREAK AT CHEZ ROMEO!
HE'S BEEN PLAYING ME FOR A FOOL!
SOB!
NICKY!
I CAN'T WAIT TO TELL VANILLA ABOUT IT! HEE! HEE!
COME ON, OPEN UP!
KNOCK KNOCK
DON'T DO THIS, NICKY!
THERE MUST'VE BEEN A MISUNDERSTANDING!
LEAVE HER ALONE! SHE NEEDS TO LET OFF SOME STEAM!
WHAT A CAD!
CHAMPIONS ARE USED TO HAVING GIRLS THROW THEMSELVES AT THEM!
THE THEA SISTERS ARE WRONG, BUT IT DOESN'T LOOK GOOD FOR GARY. SO...
NICKY'S NOT ANSWERING HER CELL PHONE! WHERE IS SHE? I DON'T UNDERSTAND! WHAT COULD HAVE HAPPENED?

NICKY'S NOT THE ONLY PERSON AT MOUSEFORD ACADEMY WHO FEELS BETRAYED...
NOW HE'S SENDING ME ROSES?! HE STILL HASN'T FIGURED OUT THAT I DON'T WANT TO BE HIS CHEF!
GIMME THAT!
OOPS!
WATCH AND TELL HIM EXACTLY WHAT MISS WHALE DID TO HIS ROSES!
BUT...
HA! HA! HA!
STOMP
STOMP
STOMP
THERE WE GO!
UM, REALLY...
...THE FLOWERS WERE FOR A CERTAIN MISS NICKY!
xNicky
-GULP!- OH, HEAVENS! WHAT KIND OF A MESS HAVE I MADE?
YOU HAVE TO FIX IT RIGHT AWAY! RUN! GET ANOTHER BOUQUET OF ROSES!
IT'S IMPOSSIBLE THIS EVENING! THE SHOP IS CLOSED!

THE NEXT MORNING, THE SKIES ARE COVERED WITH CLOUDS, JUST LIKE NICKY'S HEART...
WHY'D HE LEAD ME ON LIKE THAT?
AND LIKE GARY'S HEART...
SHE DIDN'T COME AND SHE DIDN'T CALL ME!
WOOSH
SPLASH
THE WIND IS BLOWING HARD AND THE WAVES ARE HUGE!
ARE YOU SURE YOU EVEN WANT TO GO IN THE WATER IN THIS WEATHER?
OF COURSE! TODAY'S THE PERFECT DAY FOR DOING STUNTS!
COME, QUICKLY! ROLL 'EM!
DON'T GET TOO FAR FROM THE SHORE, KID! SQUALLS COME ON SUDDENLY HERE!
WHAT I WOULDN'T GIVE TO BE SURFING THE WAVES WITH YOU!
NICKY CAN'T THINK OF ANYTHING EXCEPT HIM! BUT SHE DOESN'T WANT TO ADMIT IT, NOT EVEN TO HER CLOSEST FRIENDS!
I SHOULD HATE HIM, BUT INSTEAD... OH, GARY, I MISS YOU SO MUCH!

AROUND PEOPLE, HE FEELS AWKWARD. OTHER KIDS MAKE HIM FEEL INSECURE. BUT THE WAVES DON'T SCARE HIM AT ALL...
HE'S SO GOOD! IT'S AS IF HE'S BARELY SKIMMING THE SURFACE OF THE WATER!
OH, NO... THAT WAVE IS GIGANTIC! LOOK OUT, GARY!
GARY VENTS HIS FRUSTRATIONS ON THE CHALLENGES OF THE ROUGH SEAS!
ONLY ON HIS SURFBOARD DO ALL HIS DOUBTS DESERT HIM... AND HE SPREADS HIS WINGS!

IT SEEMS AS IF A MOUNTAIN IS RISING FROM THE SEA! IT'S A WAVE SO TALL THAT GARY CAN'T EVEN SEE THE END OF IT!
AAAGH!
GARYYYYY!
AN ENORMOUS WALL OF WATER COVERS GARY...
AHHH!
HEEEELP!
KRAAASHHH
... AND THEN ANYTHING IN ITS PATH!
WOOOOSHHH

NICKY IS THE FIRST TO SOUND THE ALARM!
HELP! A WAVE..GARY... HELP!
??

WHAT'S HAPPENED, NICKY?
-SOB!-
SLOW DOWN...

A GIGANTIC WAVE SWAMPED GARY... -SOB-... AND THE BOATS AND EVERYTHING ELSE, TOO... -SOB!-

DID I HEAR YOU RIGHT? A WAVE DEMOLISHED WINDY ISLAND?
YES! WE HAVE TO HURRY AND HELP THE RESCUERS! RIGHT AWAY!

VIC'S FIRST THOUGHT IS OF HIS MOTHER...
HELLO? HELLO? MOM, ARE YOU OKAY?

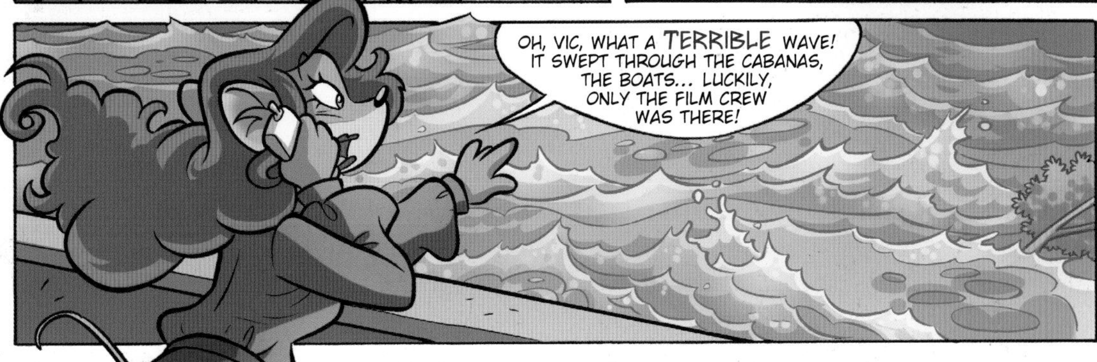
OH, VIC, WHAT A TERRIBLE WAVE! IT SWEPT THROUGH THE CABANAS, THE BOATS... LUCKILY, ONLY THE FILM CREW WAS THERE!

ALARM SPREADS ACROSS ALL OF Whale Island...
IN THE FACE OF AN EMERGENCY, THEY ALL PUT ASIDE THEIR DIFFERENCES AND RUSH TO HELP WHOEVER'S AT SEA!
TOOT TOOT TOOOOOOT

EVEN THE BIG MOUSEFORD ACADEMY MOTORBOAT JOINS THE VESSELS, WITH PROFESSOR VAN KRAKEN, VIOLET, COLETTE, AND NICKY ON BOARD...
... AND VIC JOINS IN ON HIS MOTORBOAT TOO, WITH PAMELA AND PAULINA ON BOARD!

NINE MICE ARE MISSING FROM WINDY ISLAND! BUT WITH THE ROUGH SEAS, IT'S NOT EASY TO LOCATE THEM!

DESPITE THE DIFFICULTY, EVERYONE IN THE WATER IS FISHED OUT, ONE AFTER ANOTHER!
SPLASH
SPLASH

THERE'S SOMEONE OVER THERE!
IT'S JUST A TREE TRUNK, NICKY!
LOOK!
-SPLUT!-
GRAB THE LIFE PRESERVER! WE'LL PULL YOU UP!
THANK GOODNESS YOU GOT HERE -COUGH!-
HOW MUCH DOES HE WEIGH?
A LITTLE MORE, KIDS... WE'RE ALMOST THERE!
-COUGH!- -COUGH!-
THANKS... -COUGH!-

WE FOUND THE DIRECTOR! IS ANYONE ELSE MISSING?
ONLY GARY MOON!
OH, NO!
"GARY WAS SWAMPED BY THE FIRST WAVE! HE MUST'VE BEEN DRAGGED OUT MUCH FARTHER THAN THE OTHERS!"
RNNN
RNNN
"LET'S EXPAND OUR SEARCH! WE SHOULD COVER A BIGGER AREA!"
WE'LL FIND HIM, YOU'LL SEE! GARY'S A CHAMP. HE'S GOT MUCH MORE STAMINA THAN THE REST OF US!
AND BESIDES, LOOK... THE SQUALL'S PASSED THROUGH! IT'LL BE EASIER TO SPOT HIM!
YOU'RE RIGHT! HE'S NEAR HERE... I CAN FEEL IT!

STILL, THE HOURS PASS AND THERE'S NO TRACE OF GARY...
THANKS, PAM! IS THERE STILL SOME TEA IN THE THERMOS?
TAKE A LITTLE BREAK, VIC! I CAN DRIVE YOUR MOTORBOAT!
IT'S THE LAST CUP! I'M AFRAID IT WON'T BE HOT ANY MORE BUT...
?
TURN RIGHT, PAM! I SAW SOMETHING ORANGE... LIKE GARY'S BOARD!
"YOU'RE RIGHT! IT'S REALLY HIM!"
RNNNNNN
GARY! GARY!
LOOK OUT, PAM! YOU'RE MAKING THE WAVES TOO BIG! THE BOARD'S TILTING!
MUSTY MOZZARELLA! HE'S UNCONSCIOUS.
BE CAREFUL, VIC! THE CURRENT'S VERY STRONG HERE!
I'LL LET THE OTHERS KNOW WE FOUND HIM!
SPLASH

I CAN FEEL HIS HEART BEATING!
PAMELA WAS RIGHT... THE CURRENT IS DRAGGING ME AWAY!
I CAN'T KEEP GOING! I'VE GOT TO TAKE A BREATH!
WHEN IS HE GOING TO RESURFACE?
I DON'T SEE ANYTHING...
OVER THERE!
WHEW!
RNNNNN
HANG ON THERE, VIC... HEEEEERE I COME!

FLASH

CLAP

CLAP CLAP

OOPS!

FLASH FLASH

CLAP CLAP

CLAP CLAP

FLASH

HURRAY!

THANKS, PAM! THANKS, PAULINA!
IT WAS VIC WHO DOVE IN AND FISHED GARY OUT! THE CURRENT ALMOST DRAGGED THEM AWAY!

VIC'S THE HERO OF THE DAY!
CERTAINLY NO HERO! I SAVED MOM'S LITTLE STAR! OTHERWISE, YOU KNOW SHE WOULD HAVE BURST MY EARDRUMS WITH HER COMPLAINTS!

MAKE WAY! OUT OF THE WAY! I HAVE TO DELIVER THESE FLOWERS TO MISS NICKY!

ARE THEY FOR ME?
x Nicky

OH, GARY! YOU SENT THEM TO ME!
ME? YES, BUT... YOU WERE SUPPOSED TO DELIVER THEM YESTERDAY!

PHEW!
ON WHALE ISLAND, WE ALWAYS DELIVER FLOWERS AT... AHEM... JUST THE RIGHT TIME!
HEE! HEE! HEE!
PROBLEM SOLVED!

THE EVENT SHOULD HAVE BEEN A DISASTER FOR VISSIA, BUT INSTEAD...
NEWSPAPERS ALL OVER THE WORLD ARE TALKING ABOUT NOTHING ELSE!
ABOUT THE GIANT WAVE?
ABOUT THE LOVE STORY BETWEEN GARY AND HIS RESCUER!
JACK CAMERON CULTIVATED THE JOURNALISTS PROPERLY! HE'S CREATED A WHISKERFUL OF A LOVE STORY!
EXCELLENT! THAT WAY, NO ONE WILL THINK ABOUT THE GIANT WAVE AND THE DANGER WE FACED!
I'LL ADVERTISE MY ISLAND AS A... LOVE NEST!
ALL'S WELL THAT ENDS WELL... BUT NOT FOR EVERYONE!
-GRRR!- I SEE THEIR PICTURE EVERYWHERE!
GARY AND NICKY! NICKY AND GARY! CAN'T ANYONE TALK ABOUT ANYTHING ELSE?!
VANILLA JILTED!
-GRUNT!-

VISSIA, HOWEVER, HADN'T TAKEN GARY MOON AND THE THEA SISTERS INTO ACCOUNT...
PLEASE CHANGE YOUR MIND, GARY! DON'T DO IT!
IT'S USELESS TO INSIST, JACK... I'VE ALREADY DECIDED!

THE CONTRACT WITH MS. DE VISSEN MEANS NOTHING TO ME! AS FOR YOU... YOU'RE FIRED!
OH!

READY FOR THE PRESS CONFERENCE, GARY?
YES, OF COURSE, BUT...

...YOU'LL HELP ME, RIGHT? I'M A TOTAL WASHOUT WHEN I SPEAK IN PUBLIC!
THE THEA SISTERS AND PROFESSOR VAN KRAKEN WILL BE BY YOUR SIDE! AND MAYBE EVEN THEA STILTON, IF SHE GETS HERE IN TIME!

UM, HELLO, EVERYBODY! THANKS FOR COMING!
I'M NOT A GREAT SPEAKER, SO I'LL GET RIGHT TO THE POINT...

WHAT HAPPENED ON WINDY ISLAND WAS NOT AN ACCIDENT AT ALL!
IT WASN'T AN ACCIDENT?
WHAT WAS IT?! HOW DO YOU EXPLAIN THAT GIGANTIC WAVE?

IT WAS CAUSED BY THE ARTIFICIAL REEF! UM... MY FRIENDS WILL EXPLAIN IT BETTER THAN I CAN!

THE ARTIFICIAL REEF THAT VISSIA DE VISSEN BUILT IS TOO BIG! WHEN THE WINDS ARE STRONG, IT CREATES UNCONTROL-LABLE WAVES!

DO YOU HAVE PROOF OF WHAT YOU'RE CLAIMING?
OF COURSE! I HAVE A SWORN AFFIDAVIT FROM ENGINEER O'CONNOR, WHO DESIGNED THE REEF! I CAN READ IT TO YOU...

NO NEED FOR THE AFFIDAVIT, PROFESSOR! WE HAVE ENGINEER O'CONNOR HERE IN PERSON!
THEA STILTON?!
SHE DID IT! SHE GOT HERE IN TIME!
THEA!

ONE OF YOUR USUAL SCOOPS, THEA?
NO! I JUST CONVINCED ENGINEER O'CONNOR TO CATCH THE FIRST PLANE OUT OF SCOTLAND... SO HE COULD ANSWER YOUR QUESTIONS!

THEY GOT THE SCOOP THEMSELVES... THE THEA SISTERS! MY PROTÉGÉS!

I'D LIKE TO INTRODUCE GARY MOON TO YOU, THEA!
PLEASED TO MEET YOU, CHAMP!
THE PLEASURE'S ALL MINE!
THANK YOU FOR COMING, MR. O'CONNOR!
IT WAS MY OBLIGATION, PROFESSOR! THAT REEF ABSOLUTELY MUST BE DEMOLISHED!

AND SO, AFTER A FULL EXPLANATION OF THE FACTS...
THEY'RE RIGHT!
THAT REEF IS DANGEROUS!
I'LL WRITE AN ARTICLE RIGHT AWAY!

THEN WE'RE IN AGREEMENT! WE'LL PUT YOUR STATEMENT ON PRIME TIME TV!
YOU CAN'T DO BETTER THAN THAT!
WE MUST INFORM THE WHALE ISLAND RESIDENTS ABOUT THE RISKS BEFORE THEY GO TO VOTE!

THE WAVE DIDN'T DEVASTATE JUST VISSIA'S ISLAND, BUT ALSO ROMEO GUYMOUSE'S REFERENDUM!
AND IF THAT WERE TO HAPPEN HERE?
A WAVE LIKE THAT WOULD BE *DISASTROUS!*
YOU CAN'T PLAY AROUND WITH THE SEA! WE FISHERMEN KNOW THAT VERY WELL!

I HEARD MS. DE VISSEN WILL DEMOLISH HER REEF!
NOT DEMOLISH, JUST DIMINISH!

VOTING DAY FINALLY ARRIVES...
A MONSTROSITY LIKE THAT NEAR DONKEY ISLAND? NEVER, NEVER!
YOU'RE RIGHT! NO ARTIFICIAL REEFS FOR OUR ISLAND!

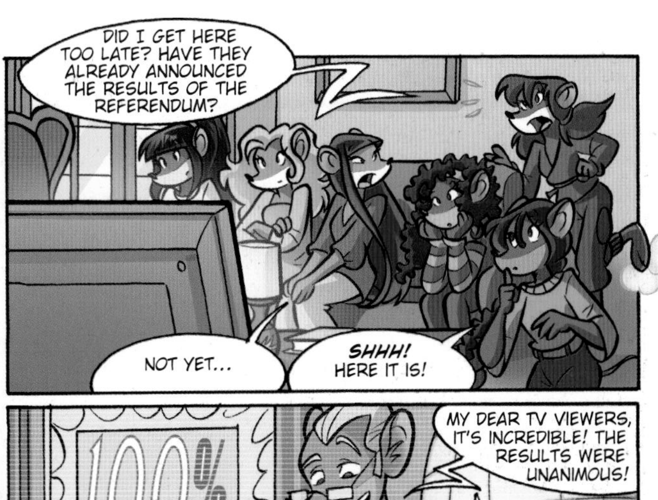
DID I GET HERE TOO LATE? HAVE THEY ALREADY ANNOUNCED THE RESULTS OF THE REFERENDUM?
NOT YET...
SHHH! HERE IT IS!

100% NO
MY DEAR TV VIEWERS, IT'S INCREDIBLE! THE RESULTS WERE UNANIMOUS!
EVERYONE VOTED NO! NOT A SINGLE CITIZEN OF WHALE ISLAND VOTED IN FAVOR OF THE REEF!

HURRAY!
HURRAY!
WE DID IT!
MARY'S BURROS ARE SAVED!
NO REEF!

HEY, IF EVERYONE VOTED "NO," THAT MEANS...
... EVEN THE MAYOR VOTED AGAINST HIS OWN PROPOSAL!

WHAT'D I TELL YOU? UNDERNEATH IT ALL, ROMEO ISN'T BAD! HE REALIZED HE WAS WRONG, IN THE END!
HA! HA! HA!
HEE! HEE! HEE!
AND THEREFORE... HURRAY FOR ROMEO GUYMOUSE!

THE TIME HAS COME FOR GARY TO LEAVE...
THEY'LL HAVE TO KEEP IN TOUCH WITH EACH OTHER LONG-DISTANCE...
BUT THEIR FEELINGS ARE **STRONG!** PLUS, THEY'VE DISCOVERED THEY HAVE ANOTHER **POWERFUL BOND**, IN ADDITION TO THEIR LOVE FOR SURFING AND AUSTRALIA...
... A COMMITMENT TO PROTECTING NATURE!
THE END

THE SECRET OF THE WATERFALL IN THE WOODS

I'VE MADE LOTS OF DIFFERENT KINDS, SHEN! WHEN WE GET TO THE MEADOW, WE'LL BE STARVING!
I CAN'T WAIT, VIOLET! IT'LL BE FUN TO EAT TOGETHER AFTER THE FIELD TRIP THROUGH THE FOREST!

YEAH...TOO BAD IT'S JUST A GAME FOR SOME PEOPLE.

DON'T TELL ME YOU'RE SCARED OF TOMORROW'S RACE, VIC!
ACTUALLY, YOU MAY STAND A TINY CHANCE, CRAIG...
AH! BECAUSE YOU KNOW I'M MORE ATHLETIC THAN YOU?
NO, IT'S BECAUSE I KNOW THIS ISN'T A RACE...

GET READY TO WATCH THE WATERFALLS FROM BEHIND, TENDERFOOT!

HE'S SO FULL OF HIMSELF...
DID YOU SEE THAT? VIC'S SO CHARMING!

I DON'T GET ALL THIS INTEREST IN A BORING FIELD TRIP! LUCKILY, AS A DE VISSEN, I'LL BE FLOWN TO THE MEADOW IN MOM'S HELICOPTER.
WOW!
THAT'S SO COOL, VANILLA!
YEAH...LOOK AT THOSE STUCK-UP FOOLS BUSTLING AROUND INSTEAD!

I'M READY, **THEA SISTERS!**
COLETTE, WHAT'RE YOU BRINGING?
ANY SELF-RESPECTING RODENT SHOULD ALWAYS BE CAREFUL ABOUT HER LOOK!
HA! HA! COLETTE, YOU'RE ONE OF A KIND!
THAT'S THE SECRET OF MY SUCCESS!
WHAT DO YOU THINK, GIRLS?
"...TOMORROW A MAGNIFICENT ADVENTURE AWAITS US!"
BUT, NICKY... DO YOU SEE THAT, TOO?

"IT'S PROFESSOR VAN KRAKEN!"

PROFESSOR, WHAT HAPPENED?
ARE YOU OKAY? TELL US WHAT HAPPENED!
PUFF...
PANT...

I SAW SOMETHING REALLY AWFUL, KIDS!

"I WENT INTO THE FOREST THIS MORNING TO MAKE SURE EVERYTHING WOULD BE OKAY FOR THE FIELD TRIP TOMORROW."

"WHEN SUDDENLY..."
GROOOOW!!

"THAT BEAR'S HURT.
I'D BETTER BE CAREFUL..."
GROOOWL!!
"I WAS ABOUT TO GO BACK AND GET HELP WHEN..."
GROOOWL!
HELP!
HOW WEIRD...! BEARS AREN'T USUALLY AGGRESSIVE...
YEAH, AND USUALLY THEY DON'T VENTURE INTO THE LOWEST PART OF THE WOODS...

PROFESSOR, WHAT HAPPENED? ARE YOU HURT?
HE WAS ATTACKED BY A BEAR IN THE FOREST!

IN THE WOODS?! BUT WHAT ABOUT THE FIELD TRIP?
IT'S DANGEROUS!
WWAAH! I WANT TO STAY HOME!

CALM DOWN, EVERYONE!
WE HAVE TO TRY TO FIGURE OUT WHY IT ACTED THAT WAY!

FIGURE IT OUT? WHAT'S THERE TO UNDERSTAND? WE HAVE TO STAY AWAY FROM THERE!
WE HAVE TO CANCEL EVERYTHING! RIGHT AWAY!

PROFESSOR, I THINK WE HAVE TO GO BACK INTO THE FOREST AND STUDY THE SITUATION!
WHAT IF WE CALL DR. OLLY? SHE MIGHT KNOW HOW TO HELP US!

WELL, I NEVER... MOM WILL BE GLAD TO LEARN THE LATEST NEWS...

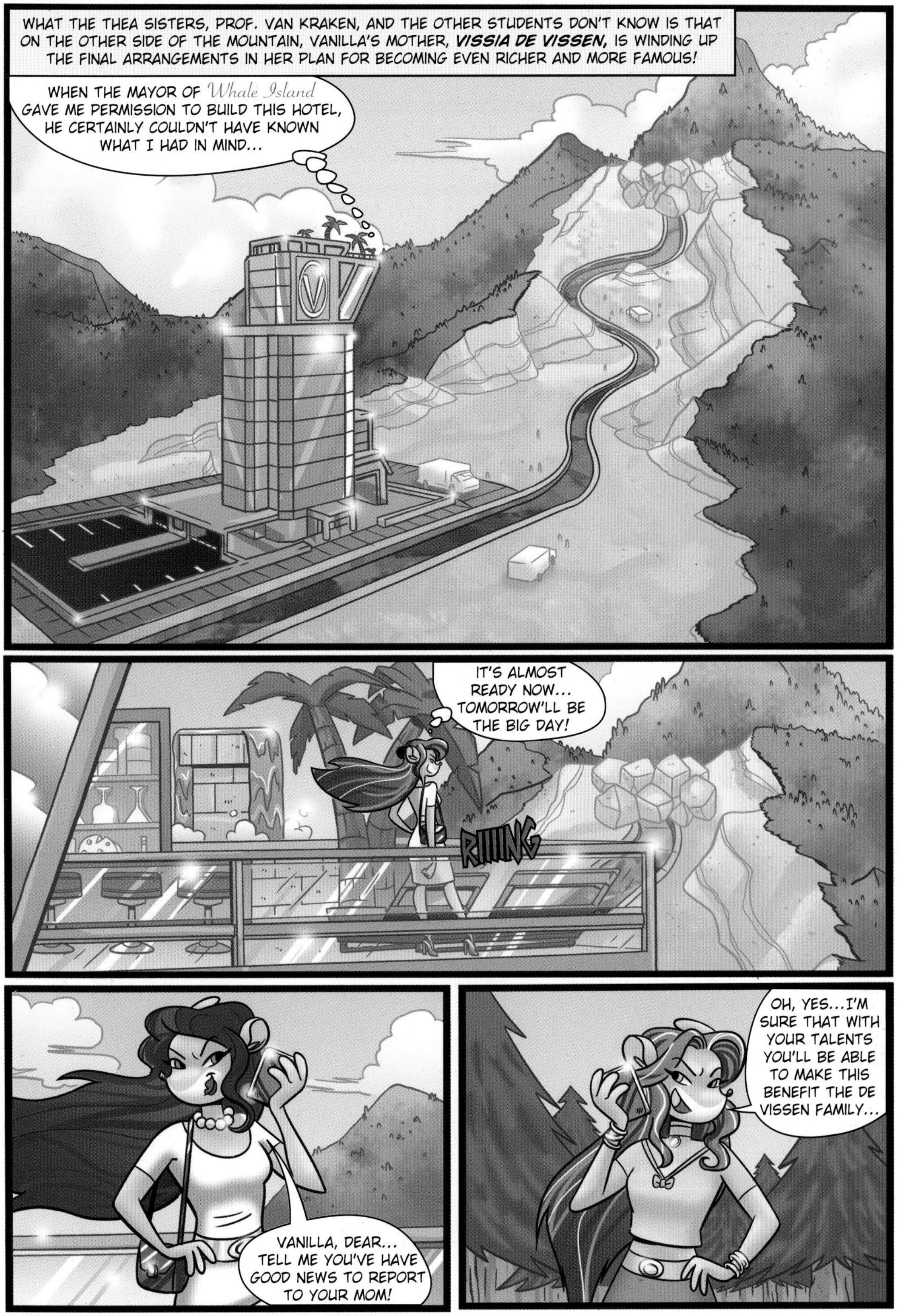

WHAT THE THEA SISTERS, PROF. VAN KRAKEN, AND THE OTHER STUDENTS DON'T KNOW IS THAT ON THE OTHER SIDE OF THE MOUNTAIN, VANILLA'S MOTHER, ***VISSIA DE VISSEN,*** IS WINDING UP THE FINAL ARRANGEMENTS IN HER PLAN FOR BECOMING EVEN RICHER AND MORE FAMOUS!

WHEN THE MAYOR OF *Whale Island* GAVE ME PERMISSION TO BUILD THIS HOTEL, HE CERTAINLY COULDN'T HAVE KNOWN WHAT I HAD IN MIND...

A BEAR, YOU SAID? WE CAN TURN THIS TO OUR ADVANTAGE...

"NOT THAT IT'S NECESSARY... EVERYTHING'S READY FOR MY BIG SUCCESS TOMORROW..."

"BUT IF WE CAN CREATE A BIT OF BOTHER, WHY NOT?"

IT WON'T BE SO EASY... THEY'RE CONTACTING DR. OLLY, THE ISLAND VETERINARIAN! SHE'LL WANT TO HELP THEM OUT!

"IT DOESN'T MATTER, MY DEAR...IT WILL TAKE VERY LITTLE TO CREATE PANIC!"

AND SO THEY TELL DR. OLLY WHAT HAPPENED...
HM...IT'S VERY ODD THAT A FAMILY OF BEARS WOULD GO THAT FAR DOWN IN THE FOREST...PLUS IT'S HARD TO BELIEVE THEY'D BEHAVE AGGRESSIVELY UNLESS IT WAS TO PROTECT THEIR CUBS...

I DIDN'T MEAN TO CAUSE ALL THIS...I WASN'T EVEN THAT CLOSE!

I KNOW THAT, IAN... FROM WHAT YOU'VE TOLD ME, THE BEAR CUB WAS ALREADY INJURED WHEN YOU SAW IT...

WE'VE GOT TO HEAD INTO THE FOREST AND HELP THE FAMILY OF BEARS!

THE KIDS ARE RIGHT! JUST REST THERE, IAN...I FEEL LIKE I HAVE SOME CAPABLE ASSISTANTS I CAN COUNT ON!
IT'LL BE A RAT-TASTIC ADVENTURE!

BUT THAT ANIMAL'S A DANGER TO THE WHOLE ISLAND! YOU NEED TO CATCH IT BEFORE IT COMES EVEN FARTHER DOWN AND COMES INTO THE VILLAGE!
IT'S THE BEAR THAT'S IN DANGER, VANILLA... SOMEONE MUST HAVE ATTACKED IT...

VANILLA'S ACTING SUSPICIOUSLY!

PAULINA, COLETTE...I THINK IT WOULD BE BETTER IF YOU STAY HERE TO KEEP AN EYE ON THINGS.
I AGREE WITH YOU... I WOULDN'T WANT THAT BULLY TO TAKE ADVANTAGE OF THE SITUATION!

THAT'S LUCKY! I STILL HAVE LOTS MORE MAKEUP TO ADD TO MY KIT!
HA! HA! COLETTE, YOU'RE INCORRIGIBLE!

WHAT ARE THOSE STUCK-UP GIRLS LAUGHING ABOUT?
WHY DON'T YOU LOOSEN UP A BIT, LITTLE SISTER? YOU KNOW WHAT I'M SAYING? I REALLY THINK I'M GOING TO JOIN THEM!
WH- WHAT?

VIC AND PAMELA IN THE WOODS? BUT THEN THEY'LL SPEND LOTS OF TIME ALONE TOGETHER!

GREAT TO HAVE YOU! WELCOME ONBOARD, VIC!

AND SO, THE GROUP VENTURES INTO THE Whale Island WOODS... THE BREATHTAKING LANDSCAPE MAKES THEM FORGET ABOUT THEIR MISSION FOR A MOMENT...

PULVERIZED PISTONS!

COME AND LOOK...IT'S A BEAUTIFUL SIGHT!

AREN'T THEY SPLENDID? WOULD ANIMALS LIKE THESE EVER HURT ANYONE...?
LET'S NOT MAKE ANY NOISE. WE DON'T WANT THEM TO THINK WE'VE COME TO ATTACK THEM...
THAT CUB'S BEEN INJURED... THAT'S WHY THEIR MOM GREW AGGRESSIVE...

CEMENT
"YEAH...LOOK...THERE'S A SACK OF CEMENT NEXT TO THE CUB! WHAT'S IT DOING THERE?"

I HAVE TO TRY TO GET CLOSER IF I WANT TO TREAT ITS PAW...
GIRLS, DR. OLLY, COME OVER HERE AND LOOK!

I'D SAY WE HAVE AN ANSWER...

CEMENT

I CAN'T BELIEVE IT... WHO COULD'VE MADE A MESS LIKE THIS?!

THERE'S ONLY ONE WAY TO FIND OUT!
CAREFUL, VIC!
CEMENT

DON'T TELL ME YOU'RE SCARED, PAM! OR MAYBE YOU'RE WORRYING ABOUT A CERTAIN DE VISSEN?

ME? SCARED?! I'LL SHOW YOU!

I TOLD YOU WE HAD TO BE CAREFUL! I HOPE THOSE SACKS OF CEMENT DIDN'T OPEN! OR MS. DE VISSEN'LL CHARGE US FOR THEM!
SHHHH!

-GRR-...I KNEW YOUR MOTHER WAS INVOLVED IN THIS!
HEY, DON'T LOOK AT ME! I'M HERE TO HELP YOU!

AS IF IT WASN'T ENOUGH TO HAVE TO WORK AT THE DAM ALL THOSE NIGHTS...
SHHH!

FROM WHAT THE BOSS SAID, MS. DE VISSEN WAS IN A MAD RUSH, TO KEEP FROM BEING NOTICED...
SLAM
BAH...LET'S HURRY UP AND GET BACK. THE JOB'S ALMOST DONE...

DID YOU HEAR THAT, TOO? WHAT JOB ARE THEY TALKING ABOUT?
WHEN IT COMES TO MY MOTHER, ANYTHING'S POSSIBLE!

AND I REALLY WANT TO FIND OUT... WHAT DO YOU SAY, SHALL WE GO?
WHAT? HOW?

VIC, STOP!

HURRY, PAM!

VIC'S RIGHT, GIRLS! WE HAVE TO FIND OUT WHAT'S GOING ON AT THE DAM...I SUSPECT IT'LL BE CONNECTED TO WHAT HAPPENED IN THE WOODS!
PAM'S RIGHT...

SLAM

DID YOU HEAR THAT NOISE, TOO?
BAH...THAT'S THE ENGINE...IT ACTS UP WHENEVER IT STARTS.

IT'S UP TO US, KIDS...WE'VE GOT A CUB TO SAVE!

VROOOM

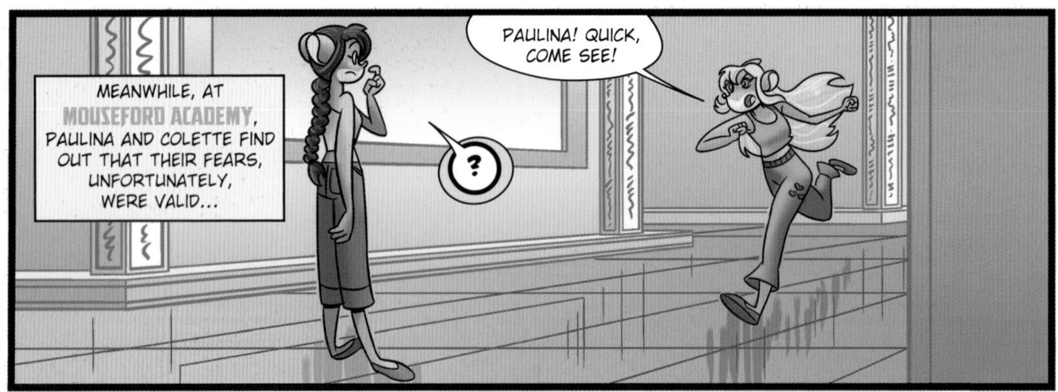
MEANWHILE, AT MOUSEFORD ACADEMY, PAULINA AND COLETTE FIND OUT THAT THEIR FEARS, UNFORTUNATELY, WERE VALID...
?
PAULINA! QUICK, COME SEE!

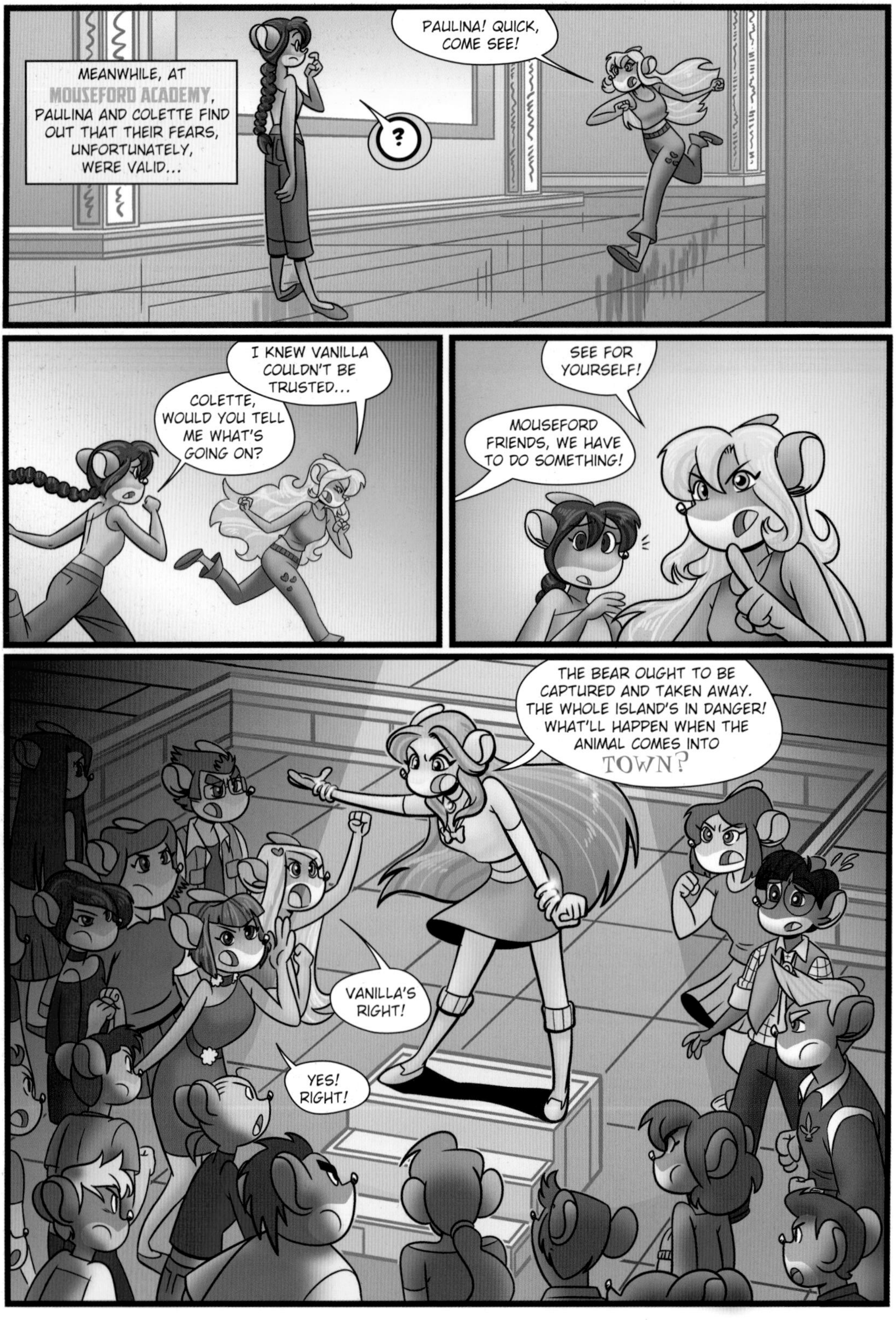

COLETTE, WOULD YOU TELL ME WHAT'S GOING ON?
I KNEW VANILLA COULDN'T BE TRUSTED...

SEE FOR YOURSELF!
MOUSEFORD FRIENDS, WE HAVE TO DO SOMETHING!

THE BEAR OUGHT TO BE CAPTURED AND TAKEN AWAY. THE WHOLE ISLAND'S IN DANGER! WHAT'LL HAPPEN WHEN THE ANIMAL COMES INTO TOWN?
VANILLA'S RIGHT!
YES! RIGHT!

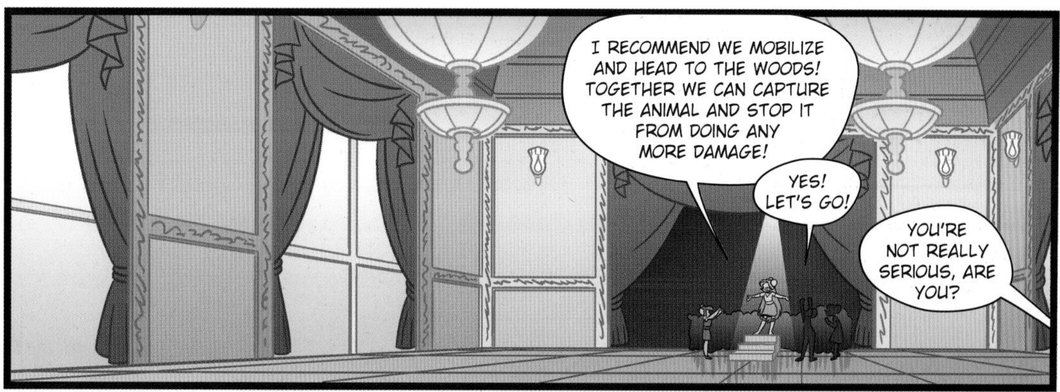
I RECOMMEND WE MOBILIZE AND HEAD TO THE WOODS! TOGETHER WE CAN CAPTURE THE ANIMAL AND STOP IT FROM DOING ANY MORE DAMAGE!
YES! LET'S GO!
YOU'RE NOT REALLY SERIOUS, ARE YOU?

THAT ANIMAL SHOULDN'T BE CAPTURED. IT SHOULD BE HELPED!
YEAH...AND MAKING A DISTURBANCE IN THE FOREST WILL ONLY SCARE IT EVEN MORE!

HERE COME THE THEA SISTERS, DEFENDERS OF THE ENVIRONMENT! THEY'RE TOO NAÏVE TO SEE REALITY...

ONLY YOU COULD THINK OF USING A MISHAP WITH A BEAR TO MAKE YOURSELF MORE POPULAR...
I'M DOING IT FOR THE GOOD OF THE RESIDENTS OF THE ISLAND! BUT I DON'T EXPECT YOU TO ACKNOWLEDGE MY ALTRUISM!
HURRAY FOR VANILLA!

NOW, IF YOU'LL EXCUSE ME, I HAVE AN ISLAND TO SAVE!

WHAT'RE WE GOING TO DO NOW?
WE CAN'T STOP THEM!
WE'VE GOT TO STOP THEM!

WHEREVER COULD SHEN'S SUDDEN CONCERN COME FROM...? AH, L'AMOUR!
BUT YOU'RE RIGHT...
OF COURSE...AND I KNOW WHO CAN HELP US, TOO!

PROFESSOR IAN VAN KRAKEN'S MARINE BIOLOGY LAB...
...USE MY HELICOPTER? THAT'S AN EXCELLENT IDEA, KIDS!

ALL ABOARD! WE'RE LEAVING!
HURRAY!
BUT... WON'T IT BE DANGEROUS?

FUP
FUP
FUP

BLUEBERRIES, RASPBERRIES, APPLES, PEARS... THIS WILL BE THE PERFECT LURE FOR THE BEAR!
IF WE SUCCEED IN ATTRACTING IT, WE CAN GET CLOSE TO THE INJURED CUB AND GIVE IT FIRST AID...
SNIFF SNIFF
HURRY UP, KIDS, THE BEAR'S SMELLED THE FRUIT!
READY TO CLIMB, VIOLET?
READY!
PUFF... PANT... I HOPE THE PLAN WORKS!

IT'S WORKING, DR. OLLY! THEY'RE EATING!
IT'S UP TO YOU NOW!
HERE'S HOPING I CAN GET IT DONE IN TIME...
GRUMPH?
DON'T BE AFRAID, LITTLE ONE...I'M HERE TO HELP YOU...
I KNEW WE'D BE FRIENDS! BUT NOW I'D BETTER GET A MOVE ON!

NOT FAR AWAY, HOWEVER, THINGS ARE ABOUT TO TAKE A TURN FOR THE WORSE...
I HOPE DR. OLLY'S ALMOST DONE...WE'RE ALMOST OUT OF FRUIT!
LOOK, VIOLET...

...I THINK THE MAMA BEAR'S SENSED DR. OLLY'S NEARBY.

THEY'RE GOING BACK TOWARD THE INJURED CUB.

WE'VE GOT TO HURRY!

OH!

HEE! HEE! COME HERE, GIRLS! I DON'T THINK WE HAVE ANYTHING TO FEAR NOW!

HAH! HAH! THEY'RE JUST BIG SCAMPS!
AND THEY'RE THANKING US IN THEIR OWN WAY!
I WONDER IF PAMELA AND VIC ARE DOING WELL, TOO!

RIGHT AT THAT MOMENT, THE VAN WHERE PAMELA AND VIC HAVE HIDDEN IN IS ABOUT TO ARRIVE AT ITS DESTINATION...
SEALING THE GATE TO THE DAM AND BLOWING UP THE ROCKS ON THE OTHER SIDE...

...WHO WOULD'VE THOUGHT OF SOMETHING LIKE THAT?
WE'RE JUST PAID TO FOLLOW DIRECTIONS...
AND THE BOSS SAYS THAT MS. DE VISSEN PAYS WELL! 'CAUSE YOU'VE GOT TO BE PRETTY RICH TO CHANGE THE COURSE OF A RIVER!

THE MAIN THING IS THAT WE'RE ALMOST DONE!
THEY'RE OPENING THE GATE. GO ON IN.

VROOOM

SCREEEECH

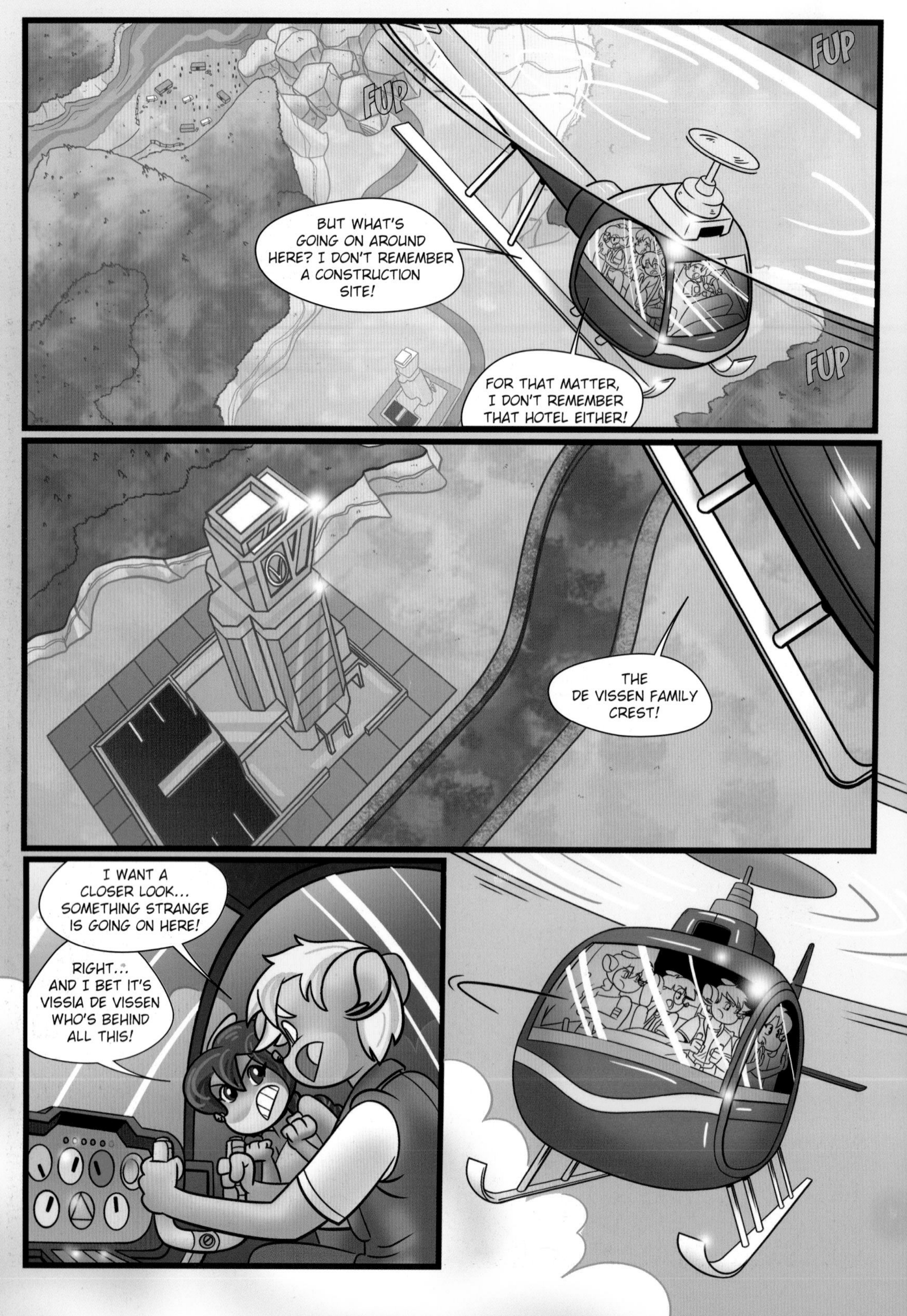
FUP
FUP
BUT WHAT'S GOING ON AROUND HERE? I DON'T REMEMBER A CONSTRUCTION SITE!
FOR THAT MATTER, I DON'T REMEMBER THAT HOTEL EITHER!
FUP
THE DE VISSEN FAMILY CREST!
I WANT A CLOSER LOOK... SOMETHING STRANGE IS GOING ON HERE!
RIGHT... AND I BET IT'S VISSIA DE VISSEN WHO'S BEHIND ALL THIS!

ARE WE EXPECTING VISITORS, BOSS?
I WOULDN'T THINK SO...AND I DON'T SEE THE DE VISSEN CREST, WHICH MEANS JUST ONE THING...

FUP
FUP
FUP
"...INTRUDERS!"

THIS IS PRIVATE PROPERTY. YOU HAVE NO RIGHT TO LAND HERE!
OH, REALLY? AS FAR AS I KNOW, THIS DAM IS THE PUBLIC PROPERTY OF WHALE ISLAND AND YOU'RE DESTROYING IT!

OH, YEAH? AND WHO'RE YOU TO GIVE ME ORDERS, BUB?
IAN VAN KRAKEN, BIOLOGY PROFESSOR...IF YOU DON'T STOP THIS RIGHT NOW, I'LL CALL THE WHALE ISLAND AUTHORITIES!

THE AUTHORITIES? HA! HA! NO AUTHORITY CAN DO ANYTHING TO VISSIA DE VISSEN!
HA HA HA
HA HA HA

→GRR←...I KNEW IT! IT'S ALWAYS HER!

DO YOU REALIZE WHAT YOU'RE DOING? YOU'RE DESTROYING PART OF OUR NATURAL HERITAGE!

HEY, TONE DOWN THOSE ACCUSATIONS! ALL WE'RE DOING IS STOPPING THE DAM FROM OPENING ON THE SIDE THAT EVERYONE EXPECTS IT TO...

OF COURSE, IF THE ROCKS FROM THE OTHER SIDE THEN BLOW UP, IT'LL JUST BE A COINCIDENCE...AND LUCKILY THE WATER WILL FLOW OUT FROM OUR CEMENT BANKS INSTEAD.
ENOUGH OF THIS! I'M GOING TO WARN THE WHALE ISLAND AUTHORITIES IMMEDIATELY!

AND I SAY YOU'LL DO ABSOLUTELY NOTHING...
GRAB 'EM, GUYS...

WHAT?! YOU CAN'T DO THIS! I WON'T LET YOU...
SHUT UP, DUDE!
STOP, HOOLIGANS! YOU'RE RUINING MY HAIRDO!

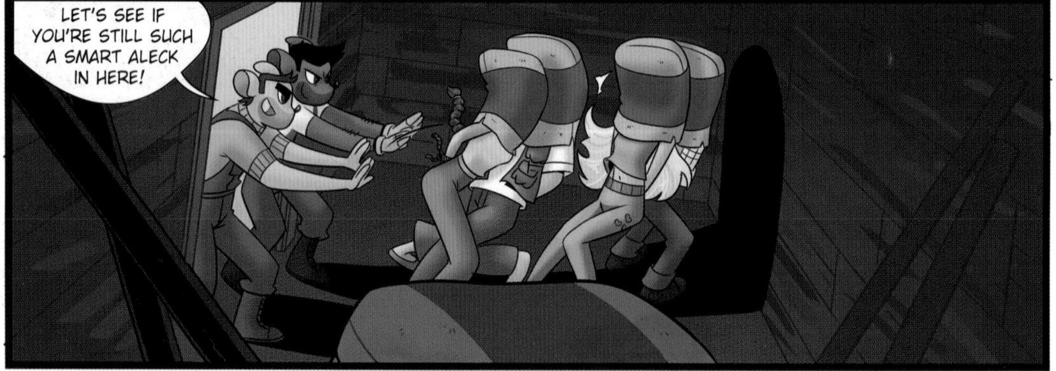
LET'S SEE IF YOU'RE STILL SUCH A SMART ALECK IN HERE!

-GRR-...THEY'LL FIND US, AND THEN IT'LL GO WORSE FOR YOU.
IS THAT SO? NO ONE'S PAID ANY ATTENTION TO THIS CONSTRUCTION SITE FOR WEEKS...

...MS. DE VISSEN REALLY THOUGHT OF EVERYTHING! AND YOU'RE NOT GOING TO PUT A SPIKE IN HER WHEEL!

SLAM
I'M SORRY, KIDS...I DIDN'T MEAN TO DRAG YOU INTO THIS...
IT'S NOT YOUR FAULT, PROFESSOR... THOSE CRIMINALS MUST BE STOPPED!
YEAH...WHO'S GOING TO WARN THE OTHERS THAT THE BEARS ARE IN DANGER NOW?

MEANWHILE, IN THE WOODS, ***NICKY*** AND ***VIOLET*** DON'T REALIZE THE DANGER COMING THEIR WAY...
DO YOU HEAR THOSE VOICES, ***NICKY?***
WITH THIS SUPER FRUIT-FEAST, OUR FRIEND WILL BE BACK TO HIS OLD SELF IN A HURRY!

THEY SEEM FAMILIAR TO ME...

WHAT IN THE WORLD?
GASP!

COME ON, FRIENDS! WHEN WE FIND THE BEARS, WE HAVE TO BE READY TO CATCH THEM!
BUT DIDN'T VANILLA SAY SHE WOULDN'T WALK THROUGH THE FOREST?
IT'S OBVIOUS THAT HER ALTRUISM TRUMPS ANY KIND OF LAZINESS! HEE-HEE!

WE HAVE TO LET DR. OLLY KNOW!

THE BEARS ARE IN DANGER! THEY HAVE TO LEAVE!
WHAT?

CAPTURE THE BEARS?! HOW COULD THEY THINK OF DOING SOMETHING LIKE THAT?

IT HAS TO BE VANILLA'S IDEA!

"EXACTLY RIGHT, MY DEAR!"

THOSE ANIMALS MUST BE STOPPED! THE WHOLE ISLAND'S IN DANGER!

IF YOU THINK WE'RE GOING TO LET YOU DO THAT, YOU'RE MAKING A BIG MISTAKE!
THINK ABOUT IT, MY DEAR...HOW MUCH OF A CHANCE DO YOU THINK YOU HAVE?

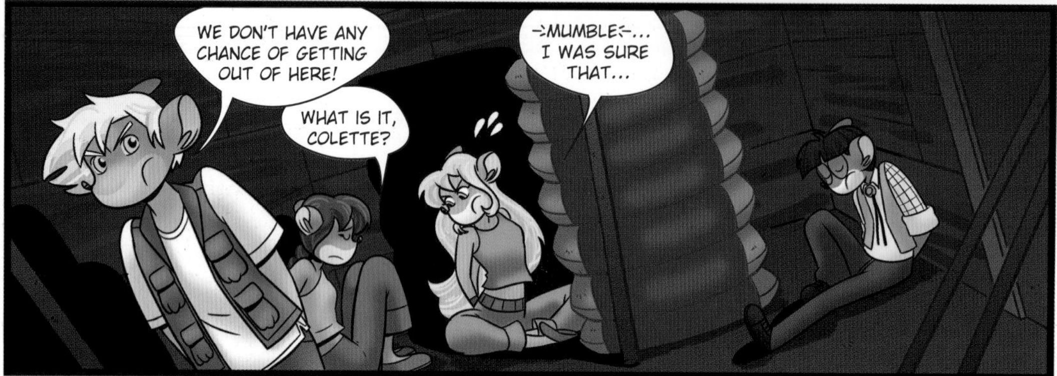
WE DON'T HAVE ANY CHANCE OF GETTING OUT OF HERE!
WHAT IS IT, COLETTE?
-MUMBLE-... I WAS SURE THAT...

AH-HA! I KNEW IT! LUCKILY I HADN'T FINISHED PACKING MY MAKEUP BAG YET.

COME OVER HERE, PAULINA! IT'S TIME FOR A TOTAL MANICURE!
HAH! HAH! YOU'RE A GENIUS, COLETTE!

WELL DONE, KIDS! NOW LET'S TELL SOMEONE ABOUT THOSE RODENTS!

SLAM
HEY, YOU! WHERE DO YOU THINK YOU'RE GOING?

YOU CAN'T DETAIN US! IT'S ILLEGAL!
SHUT UP AND FOLLOW US!
WITHOUT ANY FUSSING!

WHERE'RE YOU TAKING US?
YOU'LL FIND OUT SOON...AND YOU'RE NOT GOING TO LIKE IT AT ALL!

WE HAVE TO BRING THE PRISONERS INSIDE...ORDERS OF THE BOSS...

MEH, DOESN'T MATTER TO ME... JUST GO ON IN...

BUT...WHAT IS THIS PLACE?
WHY'D YOU BRING US HERE?

IT'S US!
WHAT?!

WE GOT HERE BY FOLLOWING THOSE TWO WORKERS... WE WERE THERE WHEN THEY TOOK YOU PRISONER, AND WE DECIDED TO WAIT FOR THE BEST MOMENT TO FREE YOU!

YEAH...VIC'S IDEA TO DISGUISE OURSELVES AS WORKERS WAS BRILLIANT, TO SAY THE LEAST!
WE'VE GOT TO MAKE THOSE CROOKS PAY!
GRR!

AT THE MOMENT WE HAVE ANOTHER PROBLEM... WE EAVESDROPPED ON THE WORKERS AND DISCOVERED THAT THEY INTEND TO SEAL THIS SIDE OF THE DAM.
AND BLOW UP THE ROCKS ON THE OTHER SIDE.

TO DO THAT WITH JUST THE RIGHT TIMING, THEY'RE USING A COMPUTER TO RUN A PROGRAM THAT WILL LOCK THE GATE AND SET OFF THE DETONATOR...

"...THIS ONE."
00:03:30

BUT...THAT'S A COUNTDOWN!
THE ROCKS ARE GOING TO BLOW UP IN THREE MINUTES!
PAULINA, SHEN, YOU'RE COMPUTER NERDS...CAN YOU STOP THE TIMER?

WE DON'T HAVE MUCH TIME, BUT...
WE'LL DO OUR BEST!

NOT SO FAST, BRATS!
SLAM

I DON'T KNOW HOW YOU GOT FREE, BUT I'M NOT GOING TO LET YOU SPOIL EVERYTHING!

I'M WARNING YOU, I'M NOT PUTTING UP WITH ANY MORE OF YOUR ABUSE...
OH, YEAH? AND WHAT DO YOU INTEND TO DO?

MAYBE YOU'RE MISSING SOMETHING VERY OBVIOUS HERE...YOU'RE SURROUNDED!

NOT TO RUSH YOU, KIDS, BUT...THE WHOLE SITUATION HERE ISN'T GOING SO GREAT!
HANG ON A MOMENT, PAMELA! WE NEED TIME!

TIME?! WE DON'T HAVE ANY TIME!
WE MAY HAVE FIGURED OUT WHAT TO DO...

GUYS, COME ON...YOU PROBABLY WON'T WANT ME TO TELL MOM YOU HELD ME PRISONER HERE!
MOM?!

ALLOW ME TO INTRODUCE MYSELF...I'M VIC DE VISSEN...DOES THAT NAME TELL YOU ANYTHING?
WHAT? YOU'RE VISSIA DE VISSEN'S SON?
IN PERSON!

WHAT IS THIS, A JOKE?
WHAT'RE WE GOING TO DO?

EVERYTHING I DO IS ALWAYS FOR THE GOOD OF WHALE ISLAND AND ITS RESIDENTS...

WHAT'RE YOU REFERRING TO, MS. DE VISSEN?
CAN YOU GIVE US A HEADS-UP?
HERE WE GO...

YOU SHOULDN'T HAVE LONG TO WAIT, MY FRIENDS...

I'M ABOUT TO SHOW YOU SOMETHING EXTRAORDINARY...

"...WHAT WOULD YOU THINK IF I TOLD YOU THAT THE FAMOUS Whale Island WATERFALL IS ABOUT TO FLOW DOWN THIS SIDE OF THE MOUNTAIN?"

I DON'T BELIEVE IT! WHO CAN TELL IF HE'S REALLY MS. DE VISSEN'S SON?
YOU'RE RIGHT! SOMETIMES WE DON'T BELIEVE IT EITHER!
HEY, WHAT...?!
I KNOW A TEACHER SHOULDN'T ENCOURAGE THIS, BUT...WELL DONE, COLETTE!
YOU BACK THERE! DO SOMETHING! HELP ME!
WELL, ACTUALLY...I'M BEGINNING TO THINK THEY'RE RIGHT, BOSS...
YEAH...I NEVER LIKED THE IDEA OF DESTROYING THE DAM...
WELL SAID! I KNEW WE'D BE ABLE TO GET YOU TO THINK IT OVER!
SO? WHAT'RE YOU DOING? WELL? DID YOU DO IT? HEY? ARE WE SAFE? HEY?
PAMELA, IF YOU KEEP THAT UP, IT'LL ALL BLOW UP JUST FROM YOUR NERVES!
PAULINA, LOOK...
WE'VE GOT TO STOP THE COUNTDOWN... NOW!
00:00:10

THIS IS TOTALLY CRAZY! CAPTURING A FAMILY OF BEARS?!

IT'S ABSURD! HOW COULD YOU HAVE GONE ALONG WITH VANILLA'S PLAN?
UM...WELL, TO TELL THE TRUTH, WE...

"I HAD NO IDEA VIOLET COULD BE SO TOUGH!"
WHEN IT COMES TO DEFENDING NATURE, THE THEA SISTERS AREN'T AFRAID OF ANYTHING!

DON'T BE SCARED, LITTLE ONE...NO ONE'S GOING TO HURT YOU!

OKAY, THIS CHITCHAT HAS GONE ON TOO LONG...LET ME THROUGH!
HEY!
WHUMP

WAIT AND SEE!

THAT'S ENOUGH, VANILLA!

NOW, PAULINA!
I DON'T WANT TO WATCH!
CLICK

00:00:00

WHAT...?!

RUUUUUMBLE

RUUUUUMBLE

RUUUUUMBLE

RUUUUUMBLE

UM...WHEN EXACTLY SHOULD IT HAPPEN?
JUDGING FROM THE NOISE, I'D SAY THAT WATER'S FLOWING DOWN THE WATERFALL...ON THE OTHER SIDE!

HOLD ON, JUST A MINUTE... SUCH IMPATIENCE! THIS IS JUST ALL PART OF THE BEAUTY OF LIVE COVERAGE!
RIIING RIIING

I HOPE YOU HAVE A GOOD EXPLANATION, VANILLA! WHY IS THE ROCK WALL STILL INTACT? I'M MAKING A BAD IMPRESSION!

SOMEONE MUST HAVE INTERFERED WITH THE WATERFALL! AND I BET IT WAS THOSE STUCK-UP THEA SISTERS...

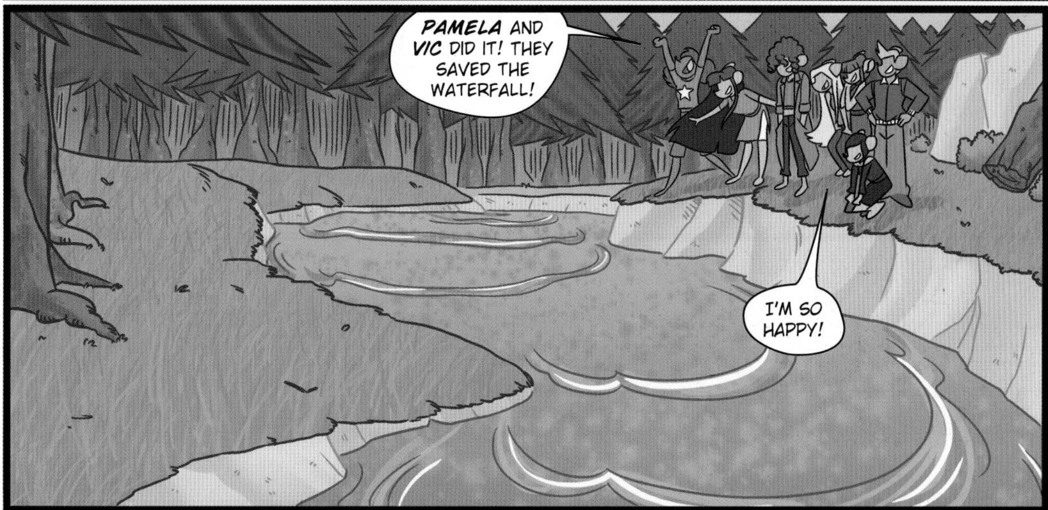
PAMELA AND VIC DID IT! THEY SAVED THE WATERFALL!
I'M SO HAPPY!

IT WAS A PERFECT PLAN, AND YOU LET THEM RUIN IT!
MOMMY DEAREST, THAT'S EXACTLY WHY I WAS CALLING YOU...GET YOUR HELICOPTER AND BRING THE JOURNALISTS HERE...

"...THE DE VISSEN FAMILY WILL SAVE WHALE ISLAND FROM EXTREMELY DANGEROUS BEARS...WE'LL BE HEROES IN THE PRESS!"
FUP
FUP
FUP

I KNEW WE'D FIND YOU HERE...RIGHT WHERE I SPOTTED THE BEAR CUB!
CIAO, KIDS! GREAT TO SEE YOU!

WE HAVE SO MUCH TO TELL YOU!
I CAN'T WAIT TO CATCH UP WITH YOU!

OH, YES... ESPECIALLY HOW THEY CAN COUNT ON THE HELP OF TWO ADMIRERS! ISN'T THAT SO, PAMELA?
BETWEEN SHEN AND VIC, I'D SAY THAT OUR PAM HAS AN EMBARRASSMENT OF RICHES!
CUT IT OUT RIGHT NOW, YOU TWO!

BUT I HAVE TO ADMIT... VIC'S NOT AS BAD AS I THOUGHT... AND WE COULDN'T HAVE DONE IT WITHOUT HIM!

HOW'S THE INJURED CUB?
I WAS ABLE TO BANDAGE ITS PAW, AND NOW...
AND NOW THESE ANIMALS ARE COMING WITH ME!

YOU WOULDN'T WANT THE ISLAND'S RESIDENTS ENDANGERED BY A FAMILY OF BEARS THAT'VE ALREADY BEEN AGGRESSIVE, RIGHT?

WHAT BEARS? THERE AREN'T ANY HERE!
WHAT?! BUT THAT'S IMPOSSIBLE!

WOULD YOU MIND EXPLAINING WHAT KIND OF JOKE THIS IS?!
BUT...BUT... I TELL YOU, THEY WERE HERE UNTIL A MOMENT AGO!

HEY, LOOK!

INDEED...AND TO THINK THAT SOMEONE SERIOUSLY THREATENED THEIR NATURAL HABITAT, WOUNDED THEM, AND NEARLY CREATED AN ENVIRONMENTAL DISASTER...
WHAT SPLENDID ANIMALS!

WHAT'S THE STORY HERE?
VISSIA DE VISSEN WANTED TO DESTROY THE OPENING OF THE DAM AT THE TOP OF THE MOUNTAIN FOR HER OWN FINANCIAL BENEFIT...
MEANWHILE SOME OTHER FOLKS THOUGHT THAT THE BEST WAY TO HELP A BEAR IN DISTRESS WAS TO CAPTURE IT...
AN ANIMAL ISN'T DANGEROUS IF IT'S HELPED THE RIGHT WAY... AND WE SHOULD ALL LEARN TO RESPECT NATURE...

"EVEN WHEN THE SOLUTION SEEMS HARD TO FIND!"
END

SO THE PLAN IS CLEAR? ARE YOU READY TO SPRING INTO ACTION?
IT LOOKS LIKE COSMETICS QUEEN VISSIA DE VISSEN IS ABOUT TO COMMIT MORE MISCHIEF. WILL THE THEA SISTERS BE ABLE TO STOP HER THIS TIME?

HEY, WAIT A MINUTE . . . WHAT'S GOING ON?
PAULINA, PAM, AND *COLETTE* ARE HELPING *VISSIA DE VISSEN?*
YES, MS. DE VISSEN! YOU CAN COUNT ON US!

DON'T FORGET! THIS MISSION IS OF THE UTMOST IMPORTANCE!
TO FIND OUT, WE'LL HAVE TO GO BACK A FEW DAYS . . .

. . . TO THE DAY OF THE HOT-AIR BALLOON RIDE ARRANGED BY **MOUSEFORD ACADEMY!**

EVERY YEAR, THE BIOLOGY TEACHER, **PROFESSOR VAN KRAKEN,** FLIES HIS STUDENTS OVER THE **WHALE ISLAND** ARCHIPELAGO!

LOOK!, PAMELA FROM UP HERE, WHALE ISLAND SEEMS SO TINY!
WOW, YOU'RE RIGHT, NICKY!
IT'S AMAZING TO SEE EVERYTHING FROM ABOVE. DON'T YOU AGREE, COLETTE?
YES, YES, WHAT YOU SAID--BUT DOESN'T ANYBODY **CARE** ABOUT ALL THIS **WIND** THAT'S MESSING UP MY HAIR?

SOON, WE'LL BE FLYING OVER TURTLE ISLAND, FAMOUS FOR THE LARGE NUMBER OF MARINE TURTLES WHO NEST ON ITS SHORELINE!
A-A-AND THEN WE'LL GO BACK HOME, RIGHT, PROFESSOR VAN KRANKEN?

WHAT'S UP, SHEN? YOU'RE NOT AFRAID, ARE YOU?
WHO, ME?! I WAS JUST ASKING FOR OUR DE VISSON FRIENDS WHO DIDN'T WANT TO COME FLY WITH US. THEY MIGHT BE GETTING WORRIED!

VIC, I DON'T UNDERSTAND WHY WE INSIST ON USING HOT-AIR BALLOONS, WHEN MODERN TECHNOLOGY HAS GIVEN US PRIVATE HELICOPTERS!
RELAX, VANILLA! THIS ALL HAS A CERTAIN CHARM, DON'T YOU THINK?

SURE . . . IF ONLY WE DIDN'T HAVE TO FLY WITH *THEM*.

PROFESSOR, COME LOOK!
ISN'T ***THAT*** TURTLE ISLAND?
YES, VIOLET, BUT . . .

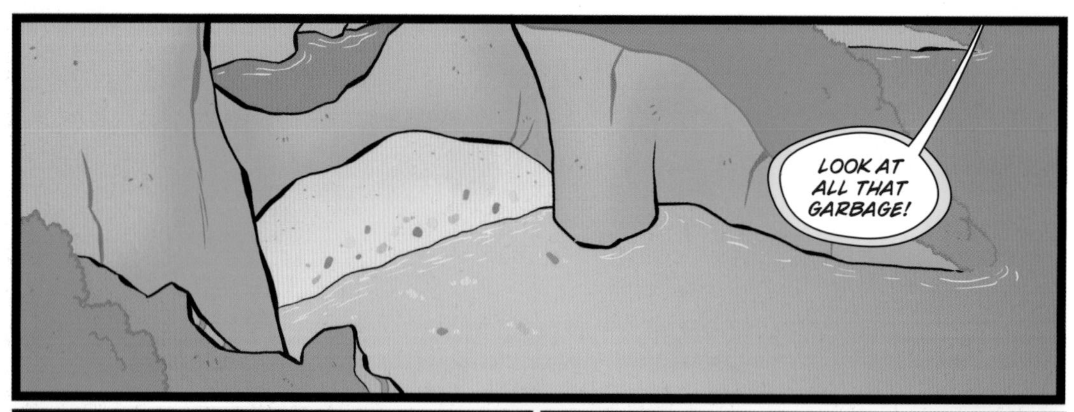
LOOK AT ALL THAT GARBAGE!

AND WHERE ARE THE TURTLES?!

PROFESSOR, I THINK WE'D BETTER GO DOWN! WE HAVE TO FIGURE OUT WHAT'S GOING ON!

VANILLA, DO YOU KNOW ANYTHING ABOUT THIS? IF THIS IS MORE OF OUR MOTHER'S MISCHIEF, THIS WON'T GO SO GOOD FOR US!
NO, I DON'T KNOW, VIC BUT WE SHOULD PLAY ALONG FOR NOW-- LET'S ACT INTERESTED!

LET'S CHECK! PREPARE FOR LANDING!

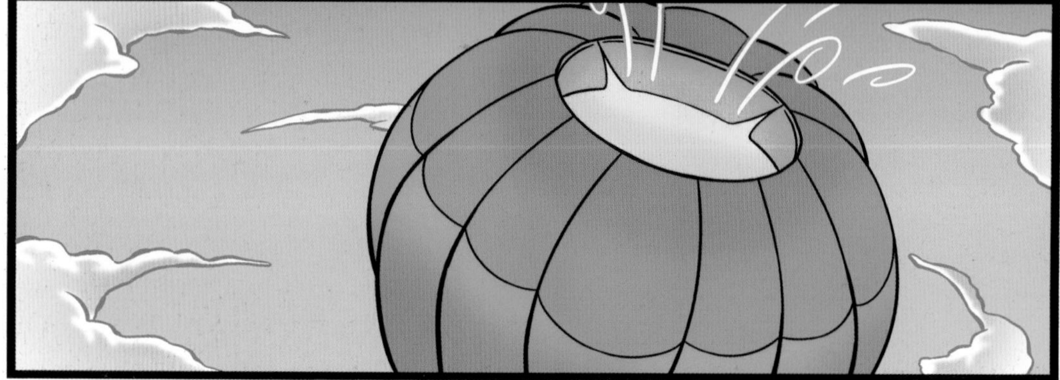

SOON...

I'VE CHANGED MY MIND. I THINK I'M REALLY AFRAID NOW!
KEEP CALM, SHEN. I HAVE EVERYTHING UNDER CONTROL. IT'LL BE A TOP-NOTCH EMERGENCY LANDING!

ARE YOU SURE THIS WAS A GOOD IDEA, GIRLS? WE'RE DROPPING PRETTY FAST!
IT'LL BE A LITTLE ROCKY, BUT EVERYTHING'LL BE OKAY!

WHAT DO YOU MEAN, "IT'LL BE A LITTLE ROCKY?"

AAAH!
THUMP

IS EVERYONE OKAY?

WE ARE . . .

. . . BUT THE ISLAND ISN'T.

VANILLA, COME LOOK! THERE'S CLEARLY SOMEONE RESPONSIBLE FOR THIS TRASH!

R.M.--RICHARD MALEFACTOR! TO BLAME!
RICHARD MALEFACTOR? WHO'S THAT?
RM

I KNOW SOMEONE WHO'LL WANT TO COME HERE IN PERSON AND TELL EVERYONE ABOUT IT!

LET'S KEEP OUR EYES OPEN, GIRLS! I WANT US TO GET TO THE BOTTOM OF THIS!
WHAT'S GOING ON, PAULINA?
I DON'T KNOW, NICKY, BUT THIS TIME IT SEEMS LIKE VISSIA HAS NOTHING TO DO WITH IT . . .

A FEW MINUTES LATER, A VERY IMPORTANT PERSON ARRIVES AT TURTLE ISLAND . . .

. . . VISSIA DE VISSEN!
WHO COULD HAVE SPOILED THIS MARVELOUS BEACH? A UNIQUE VISTA RUINED BY THE WORST KIND OF SCOUNDREL!

NOT TO MENTION THE POOR SEA TURTLES!
YES, YES, OF COURSE, NATURALLY--THE TURTLES! I WAS THINKING ABOUT THE POOR TURTLES!

VISSIA HAS NO IDEA WHAT SHE'S TALKING ABOUT. SHE JUST CAME HERE TO GET PUBLICITY!
RIGHT. AS USUAL, THAT LADY ONLY DOES THINGS TO BENEFIT HERSELF!

SET UP THE TV CAMERAS SO I'M IN THE BEST LIGHT! MAKE SURE YOU CAN SEE THE TRASH!

AS SOON AS I SAW RICHARD MALEFACTOR'S LOGO, I KNEW YOU'D FINALLY BE ABLE TO GET YOUR REVENGE.
VERY CLEVER, VANILLA.

"THAT'S EXACTLY WHAT I INTEND TO DO, VANILLA. RICHARD'S STOLEN THE PLACE I DESERVE AS *MAKEUP MONARCH* TOO MANY TIMES!"
THIS YEAR, THE AWARD FOR THE BUSINESS-RODENT OF THE YEAR GOES TO . . . ***RICHARD MALEFACTOR!***
THANK YOU, MY ESTEEMED COLLEAGUES. IT'S A TRUE PLEASURE TO RECEIVE THIS AWARD, THE FINAL PROOF--AS IF ANY WERE NEEDED--
--OF MY UNDISPUTED SUPREMACY!
COSMETICS ARE MY WORLD, AND ***MY*** COSMETICS MAKE THE ***WORLD*** BEAUTIFUL!
"NOW THAT HIS TRASH HAS SPOILED THIS BEACH, I HAVE TO TAKE ADVANTAGE OF THE OPPORTUNITY!"

WHILE I CERTAINLY DON'T INTEND TO *EXPLOIT* THIS SITUATION, IT'S MY DUTY TO STEP IN AND PROTECT THIS MARVELOUS SITE.

SOME PEOPLE MAY ***THINK*** THAT RICHARD MALEFACTOR IS BEHIND THIS DISTASTEFUL INCIDENT, BUT I KNOW THAT CANNOT BE SO.

RICHARD IS A RESPECTED COLLEAGUE OF MINE, AND HE WOULD ***NEVER*** DO ANYTHING LIKE THIS!
THAT'S WHY I'VE COME HERE IN PERSON TO ANNOUNCE THAT I'M STEPPING IN TO EXPOSE THE ***REAL*** CULPRIT!
WHAT A NOBLE GESTURE!
HURRAH, MS. DE VISSEN!

AND NOT JUST ME! I'LL PUT ***ALL*** MY RESOURCES AT THE DISPOSAL OF THE WHALE ISLAND COMMUNITY TO CLEAN UP THE BEACH!

WHAT DO YOU THINK, GIRLS?
I DON'T KNOW . . . A GESTURE LIKE THIS FROM VISSIA IS COMPLETELY UNEXPECTED.

FWUSH
?
NICKY, COME WITH ME!
WHAT'S UP, VIOLET?
YOU'LL SEE . . .
SEE, THERE'S AT LEAST **ONE** LITTLE GUY HERE.
AND HE HAS **COMPANY!**

WHERE ARE THEY GOING?
COULD THERE BE A HIDING PLACE SOMEWHERE AROUND HERE?

WHOA! LOOK AT THAT!

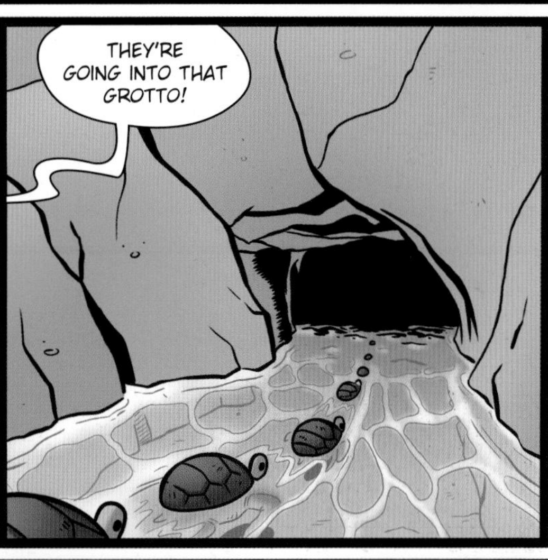
THEY'RE GOING INTO THAT GROTTO!

THAT'S **STRANGE** BEHAVIOR FOR SEA TURTLES!
LET'S TAKE A LOOK.

Oooo!

HERE'S WHERE THEY ALL ARE GOING!

AND SO . . .
WHERE'D YOU TWO GET TO?

WE FOUND THE TURTLES! THEY'RE HIDING IN A SEA GROTTO NOT FAR FROM HERE!
I THINK WE SHOULD FOLLOW THEM. I WANT TO CHECK THAT THEY'RE SAFE!

YOU'RE RIGHT, NICKY, BUT I CAN'T LET YOU GO BY YOURSELF! I'LL GO WITH YOU.
WHAT'LL WE DO ABOUT VISSIA? IN SPITE OF HOW IT LOOKS, I STILL DON'T TRUST HER!

NOW REMEMBER, FOLKS: MY ***LOVE*** OF NATURE NEEDS TO SHOW ***CLEARLY*** IN THESE ***PICTURES!***
RM
RM

I THINK IT'D BE BETTER IF WE SPLIT UP, GIRLS.
YEAH, NICKY, VIOLET, AND THE PROFESSOR CAN FOLLOW THE TURTLES. WE'LL FOCUS ON VISSIA!

MAYBE I CAN SPY OUT SOME SECRETS ABOUT HER BEAUTY PRODUCTS!
WE'RE SUPPOSED TO CHECK ON *HER*, COLETTE--NOT HER MAKEUP!

DON'T FORGET, GIRLS, WE'RE COUNTING ON YOU!
TRY TO STAY OUT OF TROUBLE--IF YOU CAN!

WHERE ARE *THEY* GOING?

THE THEA SISTERS MUST BE PLOTTING SOMETHING, FOR SURE. I SHOULD--
VANILLA!

I WANT YOU TO FOLLOW THOSE THREE, VANILLA I WON'T LET ***ANYONE*** GET IN MY WAY.
BUT, MOM! I THOUGHT I COULD CELEBRATE YOUR VICTORY OVER MALEFACTOR WITH YOU!

IT'S IMPORTANT WE ***DE VISSENS*** MAKE SURE WE'RE AT THE FOREFRONT OF SAVING THIS ISLAND, MY DEAR.

WHAT IF YOU NEED A HAND? YOU KNOW YOU CAN'T TRUST VIC--
IF SHE DOES, *WE* CAN ALWAYS HELP HER!

YOU?!
IT WOULD BE A GREAT HONOR TO HELP YOU, MS. DE VISSEN!

THE ***THEA SISTERS,*** EH? WHO WOULD HAVE EXPECTED THAT?

THEY'RE NOTHING BUT POOR DUPES! IF THEY PLAN TO MAKE ME LOOK BAD IN FRONT OF MY MOM, THEY'RE SORELY MISTAKEN!

I'LL SHOW EVERYONE WHAT *VANILLA DE VISSEN* CAN DO!

THAT EVENING . . .

SHE DOESN'T **BELIEVE** I'M INNOCENT! VISSIA JUST WANTS TO PROVE MY GUILT TO LOOK GOOD IN FRONT OF THE WHOLE COMMUNITY!

SAY WHAT, BOSS? WHY WOULD SHE DO THAT?

THINK ABOUT IT, GEORGE. THIS SCHEME WOULD BE GOOD FOR HER IMAGE AND HER BUSINESS.
I HAVE TO ADMIT, IT WAS CLEVER OF HER NOT TO ATTACK ME DIRECTLY.

YEAH, BUT . . . WE REALLY *WERE* THE ONES WHO THREW THE GARBAGE INTO THE TURTLE ISLAND GROTTOS. WE DIDN'T THINK IT'D EVER COME BACK TO THE SURFACE!

WOULD YOU SHUT UP? IF THAT INFORMATION GETS INTO THE WRONG HANDS, ***IT'LL ALL BE OVER!***
OW!

I'M SURE VISSIA WILL SEARCH FOR PROOF I'M GUILTY. MAKE SURE THIS FILE ABOUT THE GARBAGE DISPOSAL STAYS SECURE, GEORGE.
OPERATION LANDFILL

NO PROBLEM, MR. MALEFACTOR. AS ***HEAD OF SECURITY***, I ASSURE YOU THAT ***NO ONE*** WILL GET THEIR PAWS ON IT!

VERY GOOD, GEORGE . . .

". . . WITHOUT THESE DOCUMENTS, VISSIA WON'T HAVE A CHANCE OF SUCCEEDING!"
WHAT DO YOU SAY, GIRLS?

ALL WE HAVE TO DO IS GO INTO MALEFACTOR'S BUILDING AND GET THE PROOF!
GIRLS, I DON'T WANT BE PART OF A PLAN WHERE WE HAVE TO SPY AND STEAL!

IT'S TRUE. WE CAN'T JUST STEAL THE DOCUMENTS--
COME NOW, GIRLS! I'M SURPRISED AT YOU!

DO YOU OR DON'T YOU WANT TO SAVE TURTLE ISLAND? THAT'S THE ONLY WAY, MY DEAR.

WHEN IT COMES TO DOING A GOOD DEED, ALL METHODS MUST BE AVAILABLE. SAVING THE ISLAND IS A GOOD DEED, DON'T YOU THINK?

WHAT IF WE JUST TAKE A PICTURE OF THE DOCUMENTS?
OOOOH, THAT SOUNDS BETTER.

SO THE PLAN IS SIMPLE: COLETTE AND PAMELA WILL SNEAK INTO MALEFACTOR'S BUILDING AND GET A PHOTO OF THE DOCUMENTS.
PAULINA WILL STAY HERE AND GUIDE THEM FROM THIS LOCATION.

WHAT DO YOU SAY, MY BRAVE THEA SISTERS?
ARE YOU READY?

MEANWHILE . . .

YES, GIRLS, YOU WERE RIGHT--IT'S AN INCREDIBLE SIGHT! THIS GROTTO IS ANCIENT, AND YET NO ONE EVER ***KNEW IT WAS HERE!***

AND MAYBE IT'S BETTER THAT WAY.

IT'S A LABYRINTH!
YEAH, LET'S JUST HOPE WE DON'T GET LOST!

AS LONG AS WE FOLLOW THE TURTLES, WE SHOULD'T LOSE TRACK OF OUR DIRECTION.

NICKY, ARE YOU SURE YOU WANT TO COME WITH US? I KNOW YOU DON'T LIKE TIGHT SPACES.
THANKS, VIOLET. I THINK I CAN DO IT!

HEY--WHAT'S GOING ON UP AHEAD THERE?

I CAN'T SEE CLEARLY-- BUT IT DOESN'T LOOK GOOD!

I'LL GO LOOK!
BE CAREFUL, NICKY!

SPLOOSH

JUST WHAT I WAS AFRAID OF. MORE GARBAGE!

DON'T BE SCARED, LITTLE BUDDY. YOU'RE SAFE NOW!

HEH HEH!
THAT'S ENOUGH, NOW, OR I WON'T EVER WANT TO LEAVE!

OH, NO, IT LOOKS LIKE IT'S FULL OF GARBAGE HERE.
YES. I'M AFRAID THAT MIGHT BE TRUE.

WE NEED TO GET MOVING, GIRLS. THIS ENVIRONMENTAL DISASTER IS WORSE THAN I THOUGHT!

WHILE PROFESSOR VAN KRAKEN, NICKY, AND VIOLET TRY TO FIGURE OUT WHAT'S GOING ON IN THE GROTTO, AN IMPORTANT SPY MISSION IS ABOUT TO BEGIN . . .
SO, WHAT DO YOU SAY? ARE YOU WITH ME?

YES, MS. DE VISSEN!
READY FOR MISSION TURTLE RESCUE!

GOOD. LIKE EVERY SELF-RESPECTING SECRET AGENT, YOU'LL NEED TO DISGUISE YOURSELVES. I'VE ALREADY THOUGHT OF EVERYTHING.
WHAT?! WE'RE SUPPOSED TO DELIVER . . . PIZZAS?
HEH HEH!

IT'S JUST A COVER SO YOU CAN GET IN. ONCE YOU'RE INSIDE, YOU CAN USE THESE EARPHONES TO COMMUNICATE WITH PAULINA AND FOLLOW HER DIRECTIONS.

WHAT'S THE PLAN?
OH, IT'S VERY SIMPLE . . .

?
?
PIZZA! PIZZA FOR MR. MALEFACTOR!

YOU'LL HAVE TO BE CONVINCING, BUT I HAVE CONFIDENCE IN YOU.

I DON'T THINK MR. MALEFACTOR WOULD HAVE ORDERED PIZZA.
YEAH. MAYBE WE SHOULD CALL UP AND ASK HIM ABOUT IT.
AND LET *THESE PIZZAS* FOR YOU AND **MR. GEORGE** GET COLD? I DON'T THINK THESE *DELICIOUS* CHEESE PIZZAS WILL TASTE SO GOOD IF THEY GET COLD!

ACTUALLY, THEY'RE NOT ALL WRONG. REMEMBER WHEN WE HELD UP THE DELIVERY OF THAT VAT OF FRESH COTTAGE CHEESE IN THE MIDDLE OF SUMMER?
DON'T REMIND ME. I STILL SHUDDER ABOUT HOW IT LOOKED WHEN WE OPENED IT
LET'S LET THEM IN.

ONCE YOU'RE IN, PUT ON THE EARPHONES. PAULINA WILL USE THIS PLAN OF MALEFACTOR'S BUILDING TO GUIDE YOU WHEN YOU'RE INSIDE.

READY, GIRLS?

OH, I HOPE THIS WORKS.
WE'RE IN. GIVE US DIRECTIONS, PAULINA.

YOU'RE SAFE FOR NOW, BUT THE BUILDING IS FULL OF GUARDS.
GETTING TO MALEFACTOR'S OFFICE ON THE **TOP FLOOR** WON'T BE **EASY.**

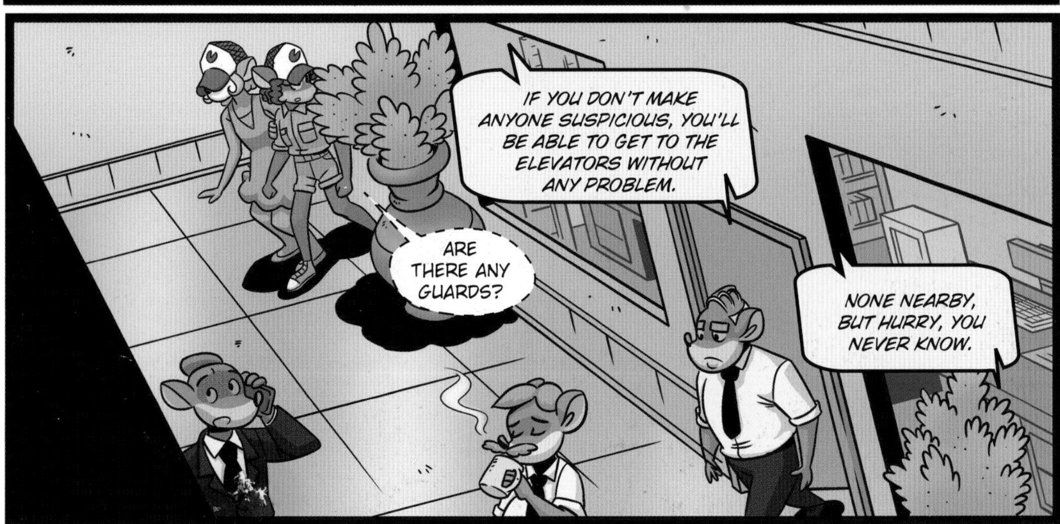
IF YOU DON'T MAKE ANYONE SUSPICIOUS, YOU'LL BE ABLE TO GET TO THE ELEVATORS WITHOUT ANY PROBLEM.
ARE THERE ANY GUARDS?
NONE NEARBY, BUT HURRY, YOU NEVER KNOW.

TAKE THE FIRST HALLWAY ON THE RIGHT.
HUH?!

OOOH!

"THE COSMETICS CLOSET!"

MAKEUP! SO MUCH MAKEUP! I CAN'T RESIST! I JUST HAVE TO TAKE A QUICK LOOK!
COLETTE!

PAM, WHAT'S GOING ON? YOU'RE MOVING INTO AN AREA THAT'S FULL OF GUARDS!
JUST A LITTLE HITCH IN THE PLAN, PAULINA.

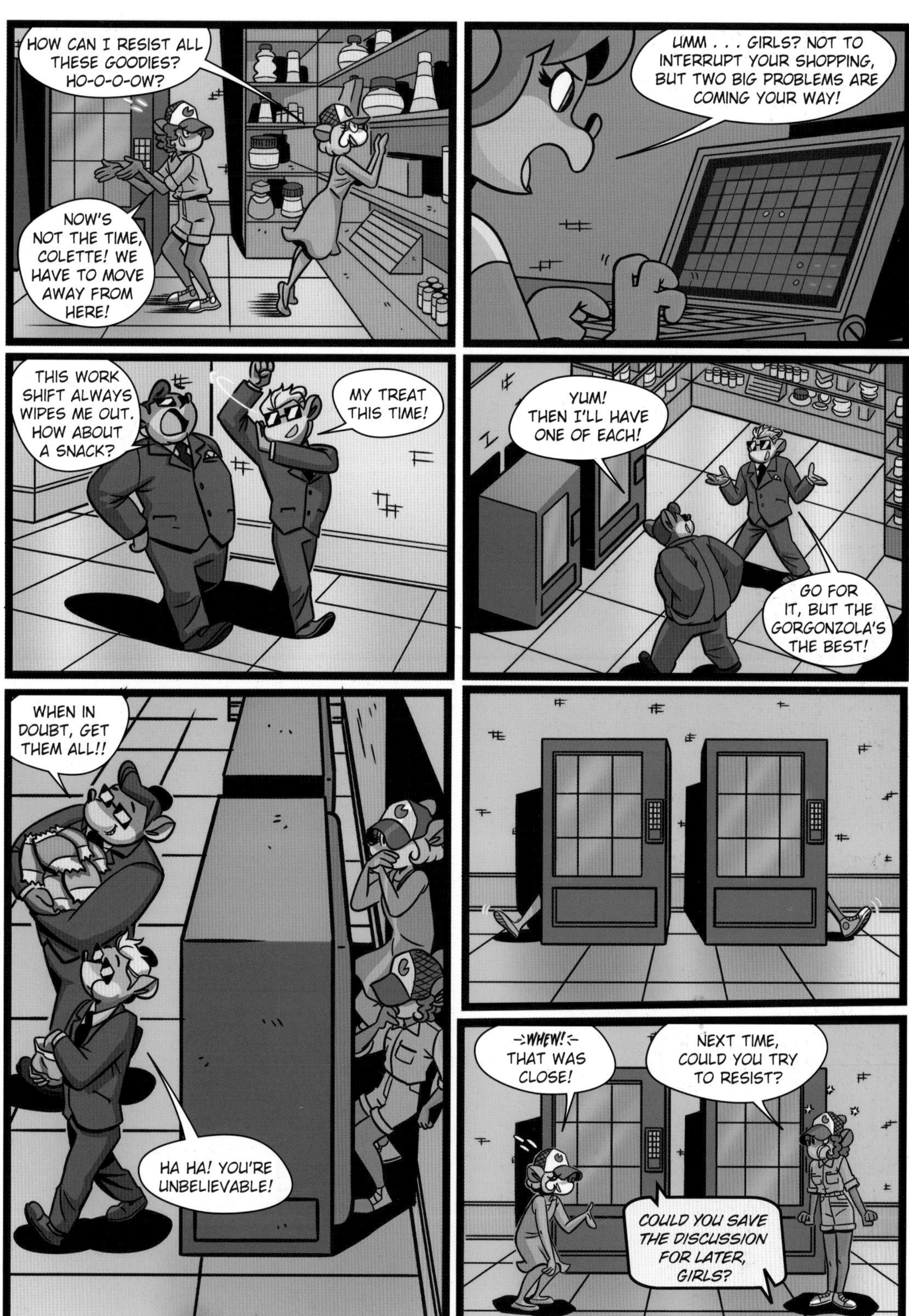
HOW CAN I RESIST ALL THESE GOODIES? HO-O-O-OW?
NOW'S NOT THE TIME, COLETTE! WE HAVE TO MOVE AWAY FROM HERE!
UMM . . . GIRLS? NOT TO INTERRUPT YOUR SHOPPING, BUT TWO BIG PROBLEMS ARE COMING YOUR WAY!
THIS WORK SHIFT ALWAYS WIPES ME OUT. HOW ABOUT A SNACK?
MY TREAT THIS TIME!
YUM! THEN I'LL HAVE ONE OF EACH!
GO FOR IT, BUT THE GORGONZOLA'S THE BEST!
WHEN IN DOUBT, GET THEM ALL!!
HA HA! YOU'RE UNBELIEVABLE!
WHEW! THAT WAS CLOSE!
NEXT TIME, COULD YOU TRY TO RESIST?
COULD YOU SAVE THE DISCUSSION FOR LATER, GIRLS?

YOU'RE RIGHT, PAM IT WAS MY FAULT. I WON'T DO IT AGAIN--
I HOPE NOT!

QUIET DOWN, OR THEY'LL CATCH YOU! TAKE THE EMPLOYEE ELEVATOR TO THE TOP FLOOR.

BIIING
WAIT!

BIIING
-OOF- . . . THANKS!

YOU'RE THERE, GIRLS! THE TOP FLOOR! THIS IS WHERE MALEFACTOR'S OFFICE IS!

I SEE IT, PAULINA . . .

. . . AND NOBODY'S THERE! LOOKS LIKE LUCK IS WITH US!

OKAY, GIVE ME A MINUTE TO FIND THE NUMERIC CODE TO UNLOCK IT.
NO NEED, PAULINA--THE DOOR'S OPEN!

OPEN? HOW STRANGE . . .

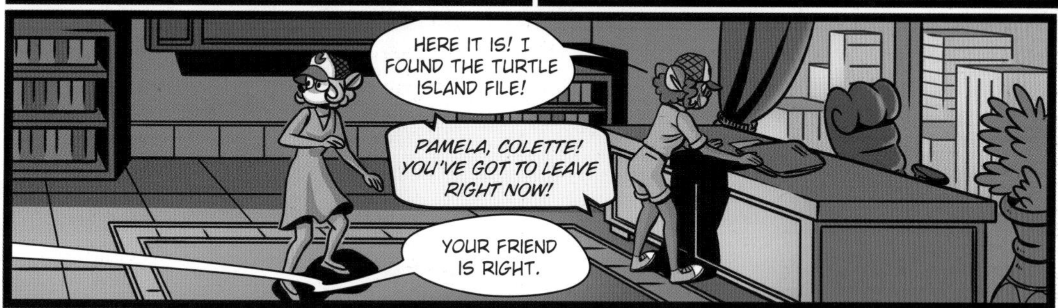
HERE IT IS! I FOUND THE TURTLE ISLAND FILE!
PAMELA, COLETTE! YOU'VE GOT TO LEAVE RIGHT NOW!
YOUR FRIEND IS RIGHT.

VISSIA, I KNOW YOU CAN HEAR ME, AND I WANT TO THANK YOU.

DID YOU REALLY THINK YOU'D GET HERE WITHOUT BEING SEEN?

THESE GIRLS TRESPASSING IN MY OFFICE TO PLANT EVIDENCE WILL BE THE CONCLUSIVE PROOF OF MY INNOCENCE!

MEANWHILE . . .
WHOOSH
WHOOSH
WHAT WAS THAT? DID YOU HEAR SOMETHING?

YES. SOMEONE'S FOLLOWING US!
LET'S HIDE BEHIND THIS ROCK!

WHAT DO WE DO?
WAIT UNTIL THEY GET PAST THE ROCK. WE'LL TAKE THEM BY SURPRISE!

3 . . .
2 . . .

AAAAH!
AAAAH!

THANK GOODNESS I FOUND YOU! I'M SO GLAD TO SEE YOU!
VANILLA? WHAT ARE YOU DOING HERE?
YOU SCARED US!

THIS GROTTO IS A MAZE FULL OF DANGERS AND MONSTERS!

THEY'RE NOT MONSTERS, THEY'RE ANIMALS! AND IF YOU HADN'T BEEN SNEAKING AROUND AFTER US, YOU WOULDN'T HAVE GOTTEN LOST IN HERE!
I WASN'T LOST, FOR YOUR INFORMATION! I WANT TO HELP YOU WITH THE TURTLES!

SUUURE. YOU PROBABLY WANT TO CAPTURE ONE, OR . . . OR . . . WHO KNOWS WHAT?!
ALL RIGHT, ENOUGH!

HOLD ON-- WE'VE GOT A PROBLEM . . .

. . . WE CAN'T GO ANY FARTHER!
NO, REALLY?

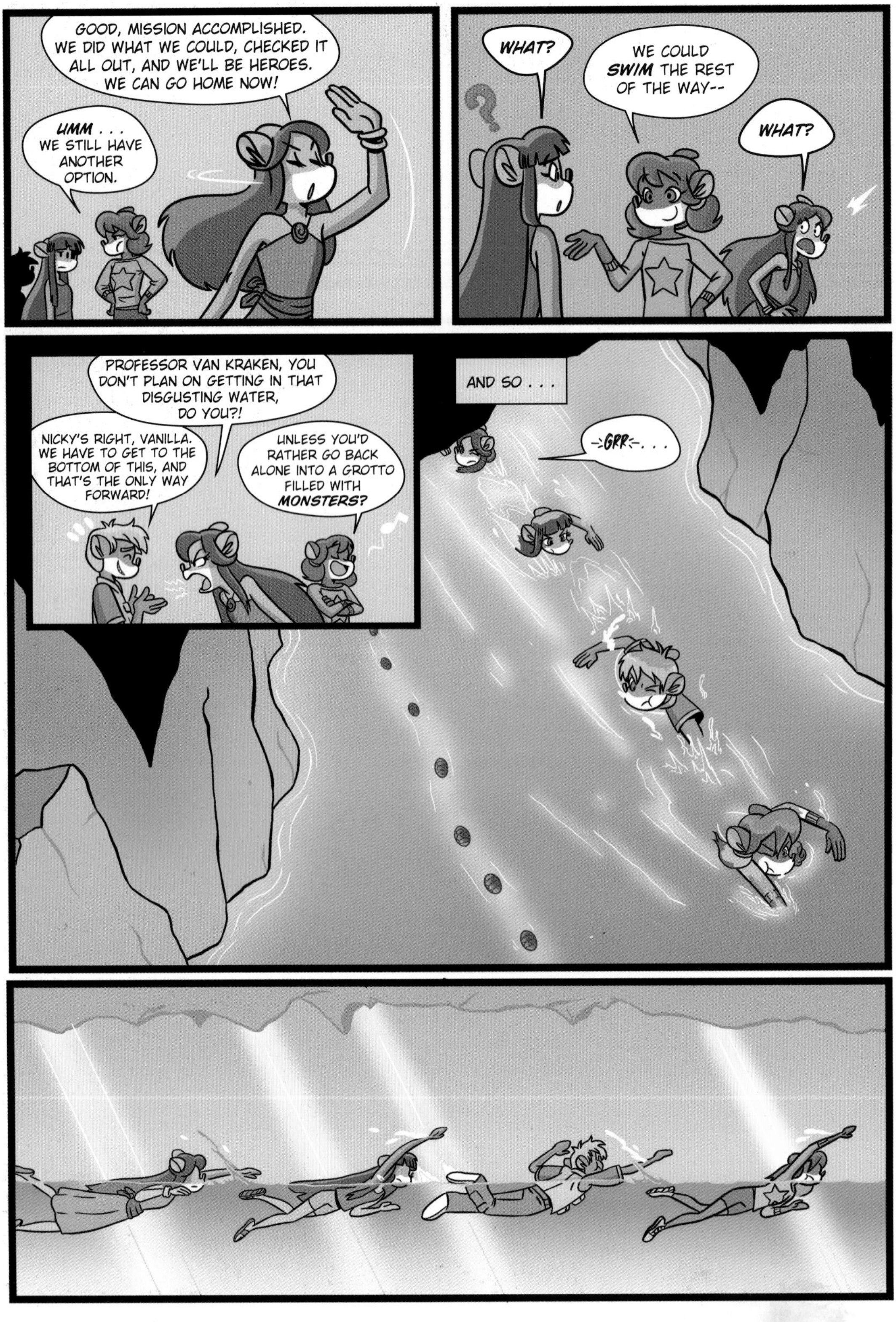

PROFESSOR VAN KRAKEN, YOU DON'T PLAN ON GETTING IN THAT DISGUSTING WATER, DO YOU?!

NICKY'S RIGHT, VANILLA. WE HAVE TO GET TO THE BOTTOM OF THIS, AND THAT'S THE ONLY WAY FORWARD!

UNLESS YOU'D RATHER GO BACK ALONE INTO A GROTTO FILLED WITH ***MONSTERS?***

AND SO . . .

-GRR- . . .

END OF THE LINE?
WAIT FOR ME HERE. I NEED TO CHECK SOMETHING.
NICKY--!

THE RIVER CONTINUES PAST THIS ROCK! IT MUST BE GOING INTO ANOTHER SECRET GROTTO!

DO YOU THINK WE CAN MAKE IT, NICKY?
WE CAN TAKE A BIG BREATH AND SWIM THERE IN NO TIME AT ALL.
WHAT?! YOU WANT ME TO DIVE UNDER THERE?!

YOU CAN'T BE SERIOUS! GIRLS?! PROFESSOR?!

I THINK THEY'RE SERIOUS.

IT . . . IT . . .
IT'S INCREDIBLE!
THE TURTLES!

I WONDER WHY THEY CAME TO THIS GROTTO.
IT'S FULL OF GARBAGE TOO.

HEY, I THINK I'VE FIGURED IT OUT.

IT LOOKS LIKE THEY'RE TRAPPED!

WOW, LOOK HOW BIG THESE GUYS ARE!
THEY'RE BEAUTIFUL!
SO MUCH TRASH. WE HAVE TO MAKE SURE YOUR MOTHER CLEANS UP THIS AREA, TOO, VANILLA.
OH, I DON'T THINK THAT'LL BE A PROBLEM.

MY MOTHER WOULD DO ANYTHING TO STOP THE CULPRIT BEHIND THIS DISASTER--

--RICHARD MALEFACTOR!!!
?

YOU ARE MY ***HERO!*** I'VE ALWAYS BEEN A HUGE FAN OF QUALITY COSMETICS LIKE YOURS! MY PARENTS SAY THEY THOUGHT THE FIRST WORD I SAID WOULD BE *MAMA* BUT IT WAS *MAKEUP KIT!*
OH, WELL, THAT'S--

AND YOU, TOO, MR. GEORGE! I'M SURE MR. MALEFACTOR WOULDN'T BE THE SUCCESSFUL RODENT HE IS WITHOUT YOU AT HIS SIDE!
YOU MEAN YOU'VE ACTUALLY NOTICED? SOMETIMES I WONDER IF ANYONE EVER EVEN SEES ME.

ABSOLUTELY WE *DO!* BUT, UM, I JUST REMEMBERED, WE HAVE A COMMITMENT ELSEWHERE AND WE SHOULD BE--

NOW, PAM!

GEORGE, WHAT'RE YOU WAITING FOR? FOLLOW THOSE GIRLS! THEY TOOK A PICTURE OF MY DOCUMENTS!

QUICK! QUICK! PAULINA, ARE YOU THERE?

COMPLIMENTS ON THE DIVERSION, COLETTE! NOW YOU NEED TO GET TO THE ROOF.
THE ROOF? ARE YOU SURE?
GRR . . . !
TRUST ME! AT THE END OF THE HALLWAY, THERE'S A METAL DOOR. OPEN IT.
METAL DOOR. I SEE IT!
HURRY, COLETTE!
OUCH!
WE'RE TRAPPED! WHAT DO WE DO, PAULINA?

NOW, NOW, GIRLS, THAT'S ENOUGH. WE'VE WASTED ENOUGH TIME. GIVE ME BACK THAT FILE!

PAULINA, WILL IT HURT YOUR FEELINGS IF I TELL YOU I DON'T UNDERSTAND YOUR PLAN?
THE PLAN'S VERY SIMPLE, GIRLS . . .

. . . YOU FLY!

CLIMB UP!
SO, RICHARD! WHAT COLOGNE ARE YOU WEARING TODAY--THE SMELL OF DEFEAT?!

DON'T CROW ABOUT YOUR VICTORY TOO QUICKLY, VISSIA!

I STILL HAVE AN ACE UP MY SLEEVE!

JUST AFTER SUNSET, SOMEONE ON A SHIP GETS THE PHONE CALL . . .
DON'T WORRY, MR. MALEFACTOR. WE'LL TAKE CARE OF IT RIGHT AWAY!

SET COURSE FOR TURTLE ISLAND! WE HAVE TO MAKE SURE THE AREA IS CLEAR!
RIGHT AWAY, CAPTAIN!

BUT ONCE NEAR THE ISLAND . . .
THAT'S NOT RIGHT!
IT MUST'VE BEEN THE TIDES, CAPTAIN . . .

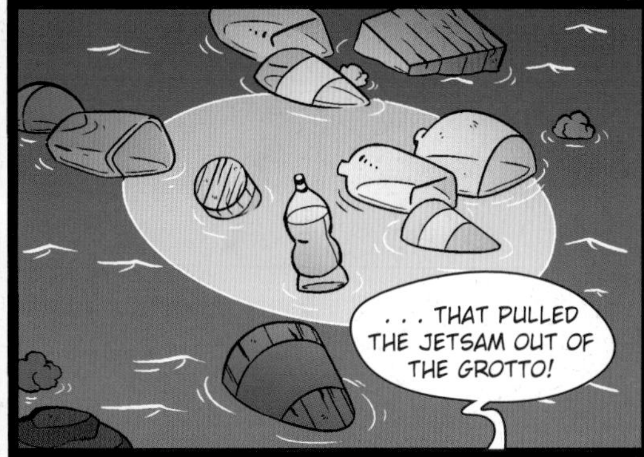
. . . THAT PULLED THE JETSAM OUT OF THE GROTTO!

HURRY! THOSE BUSYBODIES WILL BE HERE ANY MINUTE!
BUT WHAT'LL WE DO, CAPTAIN?

DROP ANCHOR AND START THE FORWARD ENGINES. IT WON'T TAKE LONG!

MEANWHILE, INSIDE THE GROTTO . . .
COME ON, GIRLS! JUST A LITTLE MORE EFFORT AND WE'LL BE THERE!
IF WE HAD TWO MORE PAWS TO HELP WE'D ALREADY BE FINISHED!
OH, VANILLA?

DON'T EVEN THINK ABOUT IT. I'M NOT HERE TO WORK!
NO KIDDING!
SHH, GIRLS-- DID YOU HEAR THAT?

VROOM
IT SOUNDS LIKE . . . A SHIP'S ENGINES! COULD IT BE OUR FRIENDS?
VROOM
UM . . . I'D SAY DEFINITELY NOT!

MORE TRASH?

I DON'T BELIEVE IT! DO THEY THINK THIS PLACE IS A DUMP?

HEY, YOU OUT THERE! DO YOU HEAR ME?! WE'RE IN HERE! COME HERE AND GET US, RIGHT NOW!
IT'S USELESS, VANILLA. THEY CAN'T HEAR US OUT THERE. AND MAYBE THAT'S A GOOD THING . . .
KROOM
KROOM

". . . JUST THINK OF HOW MUCH DAMAGE THEY COULD DO TO THIS GROTTO!"
ISN'T WHAT WE'RE DOING DANGEROUS?
ON THE CONTRARY!

WE'RE PROTECTING MR. MALEFACTOR.
AND PROTECTING HIM MEANS PROTECTING OURSELVES!

WE CAN'T DO THIS ALONE! THERE'S TOO MUCH GARBAGE!
VANILLA! ARE YOU GOING TO DO THE RIGHT THING AND GIVE US A HAND?

ALL RIGHT, ALL RIGHT! I CAN'T TAKE ANY MORE OF YOUR PESTERING! THERE, I'LL GET A COUPLE OF BITS HERE AND--

WHAT--?!

"THE TURTLES CAN BREAK FREE NOW!"

TURN OFF THE ENGINES! MISSION ACCOMPLISHED! MR. MALEFACTOR WILL BE VERY PLEASED!

CAPTAIN, WE'VE GOT VISITORS!
GRR! IT'S THE BUSYBODIES THE BOSS WAS TALKING ABOUT!

EVEN IF THEY HAVE THAT FILE, THEY CAN'T ACCUSE *US* OF ANYTHING!

ISN'T IT A BIT LATE FOR A BOAT TOUR NEAR THE COAST OF TURTLE ISLAND?
I WAS THINKING THE SAME THING ABOUT SOMEONE GOING OUT IN A ***HELICOPTER*** AT THIS HOUR. YOU NEVER KNOW WHAT MIGHT HAPPEN!

I HEAR THIS IS THE BEST TIME TO GO FISHING FOR ***CROOKS*** WHO THROW ***GARBAGE*** INTO THE WATER!
REALLY? LET ME KNOW IF YOU FIND ANY PROOF *MY* SHIP HAD ANY GARBAGE!

SOMETHING IS MOVING DOWN THERE!

WOW-- LOOK AT WHAT'S COMING OUT OF THE CAVE!
ALL THOSE TURTLES HAVE BEEN IN THERE?

LOOK--THEY'RE LEAVING!

I DO BELIEVE IT'S TIME TO SEND FOR THE PRESS AGAIN TO SEE ALL THE GARBAGE FROM *YOUR* SHIP!
GIRLS, I'M GETTING WORRIED. WHERE ARE PROFESSOR VAN KRAKEN AND THE OTHERS?

EXCUSE ME, YOU UP THERE ON THE SHIP!
PERMISSION TO COME ABOARD?
IT'S THEM!

ARE YOU OKAY?
WE'RE GREAT!
THIS IS GREAT?
AH-AH-AH-CHOOo!

YOU CAN FEEL PROUD OF YOURSELF, VANILLA! THANKS TO YOU, TOO, THE TURTLES ARE SAFE!
IT'S TRUE. IT WAS A TEAM EFFORT!

WE'LL TELL YOU EVERYTHING! HOW'D IT GO HELPING VISSIA?
FANTASTIC! WE VISITED MR. MALEFACTOR'S BUILDING!
WELL . . . IT WASN'T REALLY A "VISIT" . . .

. . .BUT THE IMPORTANT THING IS THAT EVERYTHING TURNED OUT FOR THE BEST.
RIGHT, WHO WOULD'VE EVER GUESSED . . .

CHANNEL 6 NEWS
. . . THAT THE DE VISSEN FAMILY WOULD MAKE A CONTRIBUTION TO SAVING TURTLE ISLAND?
MALEFACTOR FOUND GUILTY

DE VISSEN DECLARES MALEFACTOR FOUND GUI
I WAS VERY DISTRESSED TO DISCOVER THE INVOLVEMENT OF MY COLLEAGUE RICHARD MALEFACTOR IN THIS DREADFUL INCIDENT.

GRR!
SAVING THE TURTLE COMMUNITY WAS MY FIRST PRIORITY.

I CAN ONLY HOPE THAT SIMILAR INCIDENTS NEVER HAPPEN AGAIN, AND THAT THIS SPLENDID LANDSCAPE CONTINUES TO REMAIN UNCONTAMINATED . . .

" . . . AND FOREVER FREE AND SAFE."
END.

Watch Out For PAPERCUTZ

Welcome to the environmentally-friendly, sophomore edition of THEA STILTON 3 IN 1 #2, which probably would be less confusing if it was called THE THEA SISTERS. After all, THEA STILTON hardly appears in these stories, although her presence is always felt. To back up a little, let's start with who THEA STILTON is: She's a special correspondent to the *Rodent's Gazette*, the most famouse (get it?) newspaper on Mouse Island, which is run by Geronimo Stilton, Reporter and Editor-in-Chief.

I hope you all know what newspapers are. They're those large-sized magazine-kind-of-things that older people tend to buy. It's how they got their news before the Internet came along. Newspapers, or more specifically, good journalists, are very important to society because they uncover bad situations and expose the people responsible. Thea Stilton, Geronimo's sister, is such a journalist, and the journalism students at Mouseford Academy greatly admire her. In fact, five students—Colette, Nicky, Pamela, Paulina, and Violet—started a club, a sorority, if you will, devoted to Thea Stilton, and they're called The Thea Sisters. They're not related to each other or to Thea, they're not that kind of sisters. They're young women who want to become great journalists like Thea.

Just like the ever-forgetful Geronimo Stilton, who is starring in the all-new GERONIMO STILTON REPORTER graphic novel series from Papercutz, I forgot to mention that I'm Jim Salicrup, the Editor-in-Chief at Papercutz, the friendly folks dedicated to publishing great graphic novels for all ages.

In this particular volume of THEA STILTON 3 IN 1, you see how the Thea Sisters expose dirty deeds and fight to make everything right again. But as Editor-in-Chief, I'd be remiss in my duties, if I didn't point out something about "The Secret of the Waterfall in the Woods." When Dr. Olly has tended to the bear cub's injury, and tells the Thea Sisters, "Come here, girls! I don't think we have anything to fear now!" If there are trained wildlife workers telling you this, like Dr. Olly or a Park Ranger, then it's probably safe. My advice to everyone is to NEVER go near bears in the wild on your own. It's potentially very dangerous. Not because bears are evil creatures, but because they're wild animals. Like Geronimo Stilton, I'm a worrier, and would rather you be safe than sorry.

While the Thea Sisters all wish to become journalists, it's clear they're also good friends. There's a new graphic novel series out now from the Papercutz imprint Charmz that's all about four teenagers who have been friends since childhood. It's called MONICA ADVENTURES, and it's where you'll get to meet Monica and her friends J-Five, Smudge, and Maggy, among others. Just like Pamela has to deal with the loving attention of both Vic and Shen, Monica has to deal with her changing relationship with J-Five, now that they're both teenagers. It's a really fun and entertaining graphic novel series that we're really excited to be publishing, as it's one of the most successful comics series in the world, outside of North America, created by comics legend Mauricio de Sousa. We're sure you'll love Monica and her friends as much as everyone else. Look for both MONICA ADVENTURES #1 "Who Can Afford the Price of Friendship Today?!" and MONICA ADVENTURES #2 "We Fought Each Other as Kids... Now We're in Love?!" wherever books are sold or at your local library.

I've got a really fun job—finding and publishing the best graphic novels in the world just for you! Speaking of which, be sure to look for THEA STILTON 2 IN 1 #1 coming soon, which will feature the last two THEA STILTON graphic novels in one wonderful book! Wait till you see what the Thea Sisters are up to next!

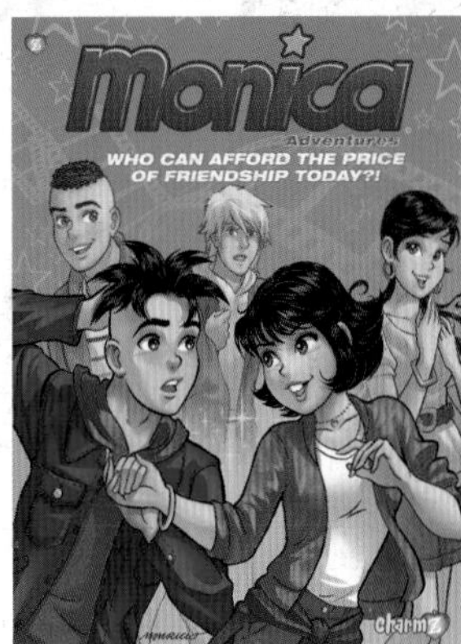

Thanks,

STAY IN TOUCH!

EMAIL: salicrup@papercutz.com
WEB: papercutz.com
TWITTER: @papercutzgn
INSTAGRAM: @papercutzgn
FACEBOOK: PAPERCUTZGRAPHICNOVELS
FAN MAIL: Papercutz, 160 Broadway, Suite 700, East Wing, New York, NY 10038

Geronimo Stilton

GRAPHIC NOVELS AVAILABLE FROM PAPERCUTZ

#1
"The Discovery of America"

#2
"The Secret of the Sphinx"

#3
"The Coliseum Con"

#4
"Following the Trail of Marco Polo"

#5
"The Great Ice Age"

#6
"Who Stole The Mona Lisa?"

#7
"Dinosaurs in Action"

#8
"Play It Again, Mozart!"

#9
"The Weird Book Machine"

#10
"Geronimo Stilton Saves the Olympics"

#11
"We'll Always Have Paris"

#12
"The First Samurai"

#13
"The Fastest Train in the West"

#14
"The First Mouse on the Moon"

#15
"All for Stilton, Stilton for All!"

#16
"Lights, Camera, Stilton!"

#17
"The Mystery of the Pirate Ship"

#18
"First to the Last Place on Earth"

#19
"Lost in Translation"

GERONIMO STILTON REPORTER #1
"Operation ShuFongfong"

COMING SOON

GERONIMO STILTON REPORTER #2
"It's My Scoop"

COMING SOON

GERONIMO STILTON REPORTER #3
"Stop Acting Around"

GERONIMO STILTON 3 in 1 #1

GERONIMO STILTON 3 in 1 #2

COMING SOON

GERONIMO STILTON 3 in 1 #3

...ALSO AVAILABLE WHEREVER E-BOOKS ARE SOLD!

See more at papercutz.com